SKIPPER AND SON

Also available in the Target series:

SKIPPER – THE DOG FROM THE SEA
SKIPPER TO THE RESCUE
SKIPPER AND THE RUNAWAY BOY

in preparation:

SKIPPER'S EXCITING SUMMER

SKIPPER AND SON

Illustrated by Geoffrey Whittam

JUDITH M. BERRISFORD

Target Editor: Mike Glover

Target Books is a division of Universal-Tandem Publishing Co., Ltd., 14 Gloucester Road, London SW7 4RD

First published in Great Britain by Brockhampton Press, Ltd., 1961

First published in this edition by Universal-Tandem Publishing Co., Ltd., 1975

ISBN 0 426 10700 4

Printed in Great Britain by litho by The Anchor Press Ltd., and bound by Wm. Brendon & Son Ltd., both of Tiptree, Essex

CONTENTS

BOATS

Chapter One

THAT NAUGHTY PUPPY

SKIPPER, the white Alsatian, bounded ahead of the hay-cart as Kitty Appleby led Captain, the big Shire horse who was pulling it across the Home Meadow.

Hay-making was a happy time on the farm. The children had a few days' holiday from school to help, and everyone enjoyed working in the sweet-smelling hay and having picnic snacks of fruit-cake, cold tea or lemonade in the field.

'Open the gate, Skipper!' Kitty called as Captain, his horse-brasses jingling, neared the farmyard.

Skipper pawed at the wooden latch so that the gate swung open for Kitty to lead Captain through with the cart.

Skipper wagged his bushy tail. He was pleased to be helping. He enjoyed the bustle and busyness of life on the farm. Everyone seemed to be busy all the time, especially during hay-making.

The rest of the Appleby family – Mr and Mrs Appleby, Kitty's elder sister Jane, and her brothers, Roddy and Peter – were now in Seven Acre Meadow. Mrs Appleby, Jane and Pete were forking the hay up to Mr Appleby who was on top of the float stacking it, while Roddy drove the tractor, pulling the float from one cock of hay to the next.

The loaders worked so hard that both Roddy and the float and Captain and the cart were kept busy. As soon as Captain's cart had been unloaded by Frank, the Applebys' cowman, in the rick-yard, Kitty would lead Captain and the empty cart back to the meadow to be reloaded. Probably, thought Kitty, they would pass Roddy and the tractor bringing the loaded float down to the yard.

Just now, though, she must keep her wits about her. She must be careful to guide Captain through the middle of the gateway and to make sure that the cart was clear of the posts before she turned him towards the rick-yard. There!

They were safely through. Pleased, Kitty began to hum, and Skipper, feeling free from his responsibilities, ran ahead and stopped below the window of the loft over the stables. It was covered with wire netting. Skipper looked up and pricked his ears.

The window was open and from the loft Skipper could hear the squeaky yelping of small puppies. He ran to Kitty's side and, head on one side, looked up.

'Very well, Skipper,' Kitty told the dog. 'I shan't need you for a while, so you may go and look at your puppies.'

Skipper wanted to bound headlong through the harness-room and up the loft stairs but he knew that his mate, Beauty, was fussy about other dogs coming near her puppies.

Beauty was also an Alsatian and, like Skipper, she was all-white. The Applebys had specially bought her as a mate for Skipper. She and Skipper had already had one litter of puppies which had been reared and sold, and this was her second litter.

As before, when the puppies had been born, Beauty was too busy tending them to have much time for Skipper. Once or twice she had even growled at him, just to tell him not to interfere. Only yesterday she had given his right paw a quick nip when he had tried to lick one of the puppies.

Puppy licking was a job for mother-dogs, Beauty evidently thought.

Remembering this, as he padded up the loft stairs, Skipper wondered whether he would be welcome this time. Well, he wanted to see Beauty and the puppies so much that he decided he would risk being growled at. He was fascinated by the scrambling little creatures and he looked forward to the time when they would be strong enough to scamper on the lawn and play with him.

Skipper got to the top of the stairs.

Across the bottom of the loft doorway was a wooden board, hooked at each side to the door frame. It was high enough to stop any over-venturesome puppy getting over and straying out of the 'puppy nursery', but it was low enough for Skipper to look over.

He put his chin on this barrier and looked across the loft. The sun was shining through the window and making a warm patch on the floor where Beauty was lying. She seemed sleepy. She had not seen Skipper, so he went on quietly watching. The puppies were nuzzling against her flanks and she was drowsily licking one of them.

Then Beauty looked up and saw Skipper. He drew back, expecting her to growl to warn him that he was not wanted. Before he could stop himself he gave a whimper as though to say: 'Don't send me away, Beauty.'

This time Beauty did not growl. Instead she let her tail move slowly. It was not much of a wag, but it was enough to show Skipper that she was quite pleased to see him.

Skipper lightly leapt over the barrier and lay on the sun-warmed floor boards, stretching his paws in front of him, and watched. The puppies were getting strong. Their eyes were open, their coats were fluffy and, when they opened their mouths to yawn, some of them showed white sharp teeth.

The puppies were sleepy now, having just fed, but one of them seemed determined to have a romp before settling down. He looked around and saw Skipper. His legs were sturdy but unsteady as he waddled across the floor.

Skipper watched him coming nearer. The puppy's little tail quivered and Skipper's tail gave an answering wag as though to say: 'So you want to be friends with me, do you?'

The puppy sniffed at Skipper's nose, wandered round him, clambered over his neck and playfully bit at his ear. Beauty had shut her eyes and seemed to be asleep. The other puppies fell asleep around her, and the puppy who had found Skipper gave a wide yawn and flopped between his front paws.

Pleased, Skipper licked him. Flies droned by the window, and, from the hay-meadow, came the slow chug of the tractor. Skipper's head dropped and he, too, fell asleep.

'Skipper!' came Kitty's voice from the farmyard below, as she waited by the shut gate with her hand on Captain's rein. 'Where are you? I want you to open the gate. Come on, Skipper!'

In the loft Skipper woke with a jerk and heard his name called again. Being a well-trained dog he wanted to jump up to obey Kitty, but how could he move without disturbing the sleeping puppy?

'*Skipper!*' Kitty's voice now sounded exasperated.

Skipper knew that he just could not ignore the call, but what could he do?

'Woof!' He gave a quiet bark as though to say: 'I'm here, Kitty, but I can't come now.'

'What's the trouble, Skipper?' Kitty groaned as she scampered up the loft stairs. She paused at the barrier. 'So that's why you couldn't come.'

She gazed at Skipper and the sleeping puppy.

Then the puppy woke up and moved and Kitty saw that he was not white all over. He was the one they had named Tippy because of the silvery-brown tip to his tail.

'So you're taking Tippy in hand, are you?' said Kitty.

Skipper gave a little whimper, and looked down at the puppy.

'You've taken a liking to the funniest puppy in the litter,' Kitty added. 'And you're proud of him. I wish I'd got a film in my camera. You two would make a super picture.' She chuckled. 'Skipper and son!'

Tippy might have been Skipper's favourite, but no dog-fancier would give him a second look, because of the silvery-brown tip to his tail and his comic-looking face.

During the next few weeks all the other puppies were quickly sold because they were fine specimens and would probably win prizes in dog shows when they were a little older.

But no one wanted Tippy. The summer holidays came and still he was not sold.

A timber-dealer nearly bought him to be a guard dog, and then decided that a black Alsatian would look more fierce.

Right from the beginning, Tippy was the most mischievous puppy of the litter. After the others had been sold he seemed to be even more of a problem.

He chased the hens and ducks and barked at the sheep. He put his paws up on Mrs Appleby's mixing bowl and upset the pancake batter all over the floor. He got into the clothes-basket with the clean washing and tore a shirt belonging to Roddy. He ran off with one of the new shoes belonging to Jane, which was discovered sticking out of a rabbit hole a week later.

He had a battle with an eiderdown, (luckily an old one,) in the spare bedroom. When Mrs Appleby went upstairs to see what all the noise was about, she found the room looking as if there had been a snowstorm of feathers.

'I tried to get them up in the vacuum cleaner,' she told the children later as they all sat down

to lunch in the big farm kitchen, 'but they seem to have clogged the motor.'

'And now I've got to take the vacuum to pieces,' put in Mr Appleby.

'I'll do that, Dad,' offered Pete, the youngest Appleby.

'I've no doubt you would,' Mr Appleby laughed as he sliced the boiled ham, 'but could you put it together again?'

'He would if I supervised,' Roddy assured his father.

'Tippy's so lovable,' put in Kitty. 'He doesn't know he's doing wrong. Just look at him now—the picture of innocence.'

After having vanquished the eiderdown, Tippy was enjoying the sleep of victory, stretched out on the cool tiles of the kitchen floor.

'Well, children, one thing's sure,' Mr Appleby sighed heavily. 'Something will have to be done about that pup. He just won't learn. He's going from bad to worse, and now he's turned to egg-stealing. I caught him taking an egg from the wyandottes' pen this morning. If we don't check him, he'll be leading Skipper and Beauty astray as well.'

'Laddie, too,' said Mrs Appleby, glancing through the window at the black-and-white working collie who was sitting alertly by the back door, waiting for Mr Appleby to finish his lunch and carry on the job of gathering the sheep that had been begun that morning.

Kitty looked from her mother back to her father in dismay.

'Oh dear! What's to become of poor Tippy then? We must do something. He may be a *naughty* pup, but I can't help loving him, and Skipper does, too. Just look at him!'

They followed Kitty's gaze and saw that Skipper crossed the kitchen floor to his problem puppy.

Skipper was watching the puppy as he slept and gently licking off some of the eiderdown feathers that still clung to Tippy's coat.

Chapter Two

MORE MISCHIEF

WHAT would Tippy's future be?

All the Appleby family hoped that the puppy's behaviour would improve, and so they were inclined to let things slide. They did nothing for a few days. It was not until Tippy jumped into a half-empty milk churn and then ran in the kitchen leaving white trails on the clean floor that Mrs Appleby tackled her husband about him.

'I've been thinking: something will have to be done about Tippy,' Mr Appleby told the children as they sat down to tea that afternoon. 'So far we've all been trying to take a hand in his training, and so he doesn't know who to obey. A dog should have only one trainer.'

'Bags me!' whooped young Pete, staking his claim.

'Well, Pete,' said Mr Appleby, 'I think this is really a job for one of the older ones. Roddy and Jane are very busy helping me on the farm just now, so I thought Kitty would be the one for the job.' He smiled at his younger daughter. 'How about it, Kit?'

'Oh, thanks, Daddy!' Kitty was thrilled. 'I'll love to train Tippy.'

'Right!' nodded Mr Appleby, passing his cup to his wife for more tea. 'You can be excused farm duty until further notice. Then, if you manage to make Tippy into a useful dog, perhaps we'll be able to find him a good home.'

'I'll do my best.'

Kitty felt solemn as she glanced across the kitchen to the wayward Tippy who was now chewing an old scrubbing brush that Mrs Appleby had given him for a plaything. It was up to her to see that he grew into a sensible dog that anybody would be glad to own. In a way his future depended on her. She mustn't let him down.

'My very best,' she vowed.

Next morning Kitty decided to begin Tippy's training by giving him a run along the sands. That should help to 'work off' his boisterous spirits. She could also call in at the public library at Sandbeach Port – the harbour town about a mile away from Sandbeach village – and borrow a book on the care and training of an Alsatian puppy.

Soon after breakfast she set off across the farmyard with Tippy on the lead. Meanwhile Skipper stopped to watch. He had been helping Laddie to take the cows back to the meadow after milking. He stood looking at Tippy who was just wriggling under the bottom bar of the gate, leaving Kitty on the other side to sort out the lead and scramble through the bars. Not a very dignified start to what was intended to be a well-conducted walk, Kitty thought, and she was glad that none of the other Applebys had seen her.

Skipper had seen, though, and his anxious expression seemed to say: 'I ought to be going along with Kitty to keep young Tippy in order.' He looked back towards Laddie who was trying his best to cope with the cows by himself. Poor Skipper! He felt that duty pulled in two different directions.

'Buck up, Skipper!' shouted Frank, the cowman. 'Bring up Buttercup.'

Skipper turned and streaked to obey. Then, as soon as he had chivvied Buttercup to amble after the rest of the herd, he turned to look back at Kitty and the puppy who were now making their way along the path towards the headland.

'*Woof! Woof!*'

Skipper barked sternly, as though to let Tippy know that he would run after him and give him a rolling-over and a quick nip if he did not behave.

Down the zigzag path that led from the headland to the beach hurried Kitty and Tippy, and soon Kitty's sandals crunched over the shingle-ridge that the high tide had piled up at the edge of the sands. Tippy tugged at his lead, pulling Kitty after him as he ran over the loose pebbles towards a flock of seagulls who were standing by the water's edge, waiting to feed on shellfish left stranded by the ebbing tide.

'Right, Tippy.' Kitty let the puppy off the lead. 'Chasing seagulls can't do any harm. You'll never catch them, so you may as well work off your high spirits that way, if you like.'

Tippy's brown tail-tip waved delightedly as he dashed, barking, after the seagulls. One after the other the gulls rose into the air and glided farther along the sands.

Tippy, still barking, pursued them. Again the seagulls waited until he had almost caught them before rising out of reach, cackling mockingly. Tippy made two more dashes. Then he gave up and pretended to be interested in a pile of seaweed.

The seagulls had sounded as if they were laughing at him, and Tippy, like most dogs,

could not bear to be laughed at. He decided to pretend that he had never wanted to catch the sea-gulls after all and that he found the sea-wet smell of the seaweed much more exciting.

'Come on, Tippy,' Kitty called after a few minutes, and she was pleased when the pup obediently ran to her.

Perhaps Tippy was not going to be such a problem dog after all. Now that he was away from the farm and the temptations to run after livestock, he seemed better behaved.

'Yes, I'm going to make you into a good puppy, Tippy,' Kitty said as she ran alongside him. 'And you must try to help.'

After a while they came to some boys and a girl who were playing cricket with a red rubber ball, and using as wickets stumps which they had driven into the sands.

Tippy suddenly saw the red ball and his puppy ears pricked upright. *Woof!* Here was something to chase. Barking with delight he bounded after it, and the children, entering into the spirit of the game, abandoned their cricket for the moment and threw the ball to each other, aiming low but just out of Tippy's reach.

Jumping to catch it, Tippy followed the ball round the circle that the children had formed. Then the girl dropped it.

Here was Tippy's chance! He streaked after the ball and pulled up, paws skidding on the wet sand, to pick up the ball in his mouth and run off with it while Kitty and the children gave chase.

'You are lucky to have such a jolly puppy,' the girl told Kitty as she tried to take the ball from Tippy. 'And doesn't he look comic?'

'Is this other Alastian yours, as well?' asked a boy, pointing to a white streak which had just plunged down a headland path to the beach.

'Yes, that's Skipper,' said Kitty. 'He's Tippy's father. He wanted to come with us when we set off, but he had to help to take the cows to their field.'

Then, it seemed, most of the holiday-makers on this part of the beach began to join in the dog-fun. Tippy was still being very mischievous, Kitty thought, but it did not seem to matter on the sands. Instead of being annoyed, everyone seemed only to be amused by his tricks. Even when he snatched some knitting from a woman's lap and ran off with it, unroving some of it, the woman only laughed and tickled Tippy's tummy as he rolled over, paws up begging forgiveness.

'You're a scamp,' she told him.

'*Grrrrr!*' growled Skipper at Tippy, as though to say: 'You'd better come and play with me. These humans aren't keeping you in order!'

To get Tippy interested in a real doggy game,

Skipper picked up in his teeth a small piece of driftwood and ran into the wavelets, dropping the stick in the water and barking back at Tippy to say: 'Come on. Join in the fun!'

'Now's your chance, Tippy,' said Kitty. 'Skipper wants to teach you the stick game.'

Soon Tippy had learned how fascinating that game could be. In and out of the water he splashed, bringing the stick back for Kitty to throw again, while Skipper tried to control his own impatience and only went in himself after it when Tippy was slow in finding the stick among the foam.

This was all Tippy needed, thought Kitty, to get away from all the opportunities for mischief at the farm and to scamper about the beach. Well, that was part of his day's training finished; now to go to Sandbeach Port and borrow that book on puppy training.

Chapter Three

SKIPPER TO THE RESCUE

'TIPPY'S full of mischief.' Kitty told a kindly-looking girl behind the counter of the Sandbeach Port public library half an hour later. 'I need a book on puppy training rather urgently.'

'Yes, I do understand,' said the girl, anxiously watching Tippy straining to scrabble at some books on a lower shelf. 'But we can't lend you one until your father has filled in this form for you. Then we can issue you with a lending ticket.'

'Oh dear!' sighed Kitty, making a grab for Tippy's collar as he started biting a hole in a string bag that someone had left by the counter. 'Goodness knows what Tippy will do in the meantime. And, oh, I say, Tippy oughtn't to be in here at all!'

She had just caught sight of a notice on the wall.

NO DOGS ALLOWED
IN THE LIBRARY

'Well, strictly speaking, no,' said the girl.

She looked sympathetic, and Kitty knew that if she could she would have broken the rule, and lent her a book without the ticket.

'I'm sorry,' Kitty groaned, feeling that this was one of those days when she just couldn't do right.

'Never mind. Put the form safely in your blazer pocket,' said the girl, 'and I'll save the best book we've got on dog training until you call again.'

Kitty thanked her and dragged Tippy through the swing doors.

Skipper, meanwhile, was waiting patiently on the library steps.

'Come on, Skipper,' Kitty said. 'We've got to go home, and come back later.'

They set off, and then Kitty paused at the corner shop. There on a tray in the window were some brightly coloured rubber balls, marked sixpence. Kitty had sixpence knotted into her handkerchief. She had meant to buy some chocolate with it to eat on the way home. Now she changed her mind. She decided that if Tippy had a ball of his very own he would be less likely to run off with balls belonging to other people.

Kitty chose a bright yellow ball and paid over her sixpence. She put the ball in her pocket, taking care not to crease the form that the library assistant had given her. Then she turned to walk along Sandbeach quay before setting off for home along the sands.

Tippy jumped up to nose her pocket as they walked.

'Wait until we get on the sands,' Kitty told him, and she had scarcely finished speaking before Tippy had forgotten the ball.

Something else had caught his eye. He saw a piece of driftwood swirling past in the swiftly ebbing tide. He gave an excited bark as though to tell Skipper that here was a chance to play the stick game again. But Skipper was too busy sniffing at a pile of fish boxes farther along the quay, so Tippy decided he would play the stick game by himself.

Before Kitty realized it, he jerked at his lead, flattened his ears against his head and wriggled out of his collar. Leaving the collar and lead dangling from Kitty's hand, Tippy jumped, *splash*, into the deep water.

'Oh dear, Tippy!' she gasped in dismay. She ran to the edge of the quay and bent down to try to reach Tippy. Already the tide had carried him out of her reach.

'Tippy! Tippy!'

She saw his paws moving frantically as he tried to swim against the current towards the quay.

'That's it, Tippy,' she called. 'Good puppy! Swim hard!'

If only he could get nearer, she would be able to lean over and grab him.

Then in spite of Tippy's efforts, the tide began

carrying him away. She glanced round desperately. If only there was a rowing-boat that she could borrow. By the time she had got to the nearest one and explained to the boatman, Tippy would be drowned. She kicked off her sandals, and took off her blazer. She knew it was foolhardy to try to swim in such a strong current, but she couldn't just let Tippy drown.

'No, you don't,' said a voice and a man's hand grasped her arm. 'You'll be drowned, too, if you try to go in.'

Kitty turned to face a kindly-looking, elderly man.

'Please let me go,' she pleaded. 'I've got to save Tippy.'

'And I've got to prevent you attempting anything so silly,' the man said, gripping her other arm and holding her tight.

Kitty wriggled but could not free herself. She knew the man was doing this for her sake. He did not think she should endanger her own life to save Tippy. Now Tippy was being swirled towards the sharp rocks at the river mouth.

She looked from Tippy towards Skipper who was still sniffing at the fish boxes, unaware of Tippy's danger.

'Skipper!' Kitty shouted. 'Here, Skipper!'

The white Alsatian dragged his nose away from

the fishy smell. He turned his head towards Kitty and saw her in the grip of the elderly man. A growl rising in his throat, Skipper bounded towards Kitty's captor.

'No, Skipper!' Kitty called. 'I don't need

rescuing. I'm all right. It's Tippy you must save.' She turned to the man. 'Please let me go. I promise I won't go in the water. Let me send Skipper after Tippy, please.'

'Very well.' He let go of Kitty's arms and moved off down the quay. 'If you'll be a sensible girl and not go in, I'll try to get a boat.'

Kitty took Skipper's collar and turned her head, trying to make him look towards Tippy who was now nearly in mid-river.

Skipper did not seem able to see.

Kitty let go his collar and delving her hand into her blazer pocket, brought out the yellow rubber ball.

'Look, Skipper!' She held the ball in front of him for a moment and then threw it as far as she could into the river towards Tippy who was choking and spluttering.

Skipper gave a quick yelp. Now he knew what Kitty wanted. He tensed himself and then sprang right out into the water.

Kitty held her breath as she watched, and now other people were running from different parts of the quay.

'There he is!' shouted a youth in jeans who had come running out of the boat-builder's yard where the elderly man had gone for help. Kitty watched, not daring to call encouragement in case she should distract Skipper who was swimming strongly with the tide, turning his head this way and that as though to look for Tippy. Kitty was sure that Skipper knew he must not bother about the ball. All that mattered was rescuing Tippy.

From the quay, Kitty could see Tippy being dragged to the outer swirl of the whirlpool, but Skipper still could not see the puppy. He was trying to look across the choppy wavelets.

Kitty ran down the quay until she was level with the Perch Light whirlpool.

'Come on, Skipper! That's right!' she shouted.

Skipper must have heard her. He looked up.

'This way, Skipper!'

Kitty suddenly stopped shouting. Skipper now thought he was being ordered to come ashore. Kitty groaned as he swam across the current towards some stone landing steps.

'No, Skipper. Over there!' Kitty picked up a stone. Tippy's life might depend on how accurately she threw.

'Watch, Skipper! Watch!' she shouted and when she was sure that Skipper could see her, she flung the stone towards Tippy, whose body now seemed limp and unresisting as it was swept along by the roaring tide.

The stone plopped into the water only a yard from Tippy's head and a cheer went up from the

watchers on the quay as Skipper, his bushy tail acting as a rudder, changed course across the current and swam strongly towards the whirlpool.

Skipper gave a watery yelp. Now he must have seen Tippy. He swam even faster.

'Oh, good dog, Skipper!' Kitty gasped in relief as Skipper's white head reached out and his strong jaws grasped Tippy by the scruff of the neck and snatched him away from the whirlpool.

Pulling a well-grown puppy across the current was a difficult task for even such a powerful dog as Skipper.

Meanwhile the youth from the boatyard and the elderly man had put out in a dinghy with an outboard motor. Another man from a yacht moored in the estuary had seen what was happening. He was sculling across in the yacht's tender. The outboard dinghy got there first, and the youth shut down the motor as it neared the two dogs. The elderly man leant over the gunwale to grab Tippy and to haul him aboard, while the youth helped Skipper who was scrabbling at the stern-counter.

Tippy looked very wet and limp as the boat drew against the quay, and one of the men handed him to Kitty who carried him up to the steps. She rubbed him with her handkerchief. He tried to stand, but his legs were too wobbly.

'Poor Tippy!' Kitty sympathized. 'You have had a horrid adventure. Well, just lie here in the sun for a while.' She turned to Skipper who was sitting by the puppy, licking him. 'Yes, go on doing that, Skipper. It'll make Tippy feel better.'

Chapter Four

POOR TIPPY

KITTY sat on the top of the quay steps, letting Tippy rest his head in her lap while he recovered. His breathing still sounded watery. He gave a few choking coughs and Kitty had to pat him between the shoulder blades to help him to get his breath. Skipper stood beside them, licking Tippy's face as though to encourage him to stand.

Suddenly Skipper gave a short bark, and Kitty heard footsteps behind her.

'So there you are, Kitty!'

Kitty glanced up. Her relief at her father's arrival changed to dismay when she saw how cross and worried he looked.

'I've been looking everywhere for you.' Mr Appleby sounded really stern. 'Someone in the town told me that Tippy and Skipper had been nearly drowned and that a boat had to go out to rescue them.'

'Yes, that's true, Daddy,' Kitty agreed miserably. She had promised to keep Tippy out of trouble – and this had happened! She ought to have had her wits about her. Then she might have been able to prevent the disaster.

'Why didn't you look after Tippy properly?' her father asked. 'You said you would keep him on his lead.'

'I know —' Unhappily Kitty began to explain everything. 'It wasn't really Tippy's fault,' she ended. 'He saw the stick in the water and I suppose he thought it was a game. You see, we'd been playing the stick game with Skipper on the beach.'

'You must have been getting Tippy over-excited,' her father groaned. 'Training a puppy doesn't just mean playing games with him, you know. Honestly, Kitty, I thought you'd got more sense!'

Kitty was ashamed. 'I'm sorry, Daddy. I just didn't think.'

'Well, I suppose we can't expect old heads on young shoulders,' Mr Appleby said, sounding less angry now that he could see Kitty realized the seriousness of what had happened. He patted his daughter's shoulder before bending gently to pick up Tippy. 'Come on, chick. We'd best get Tippy to the farm.'

The puppy's head lolled helplessly as Mr Appleby carried him to the van and laid him in the back on some empty sacks. Skipper jumped in beside him, and Mr Appleby headed for home with Kitty craning over the seat to watch Tippy.

At Headland Farm the other Applebys fussed round Tippy when he was carried into the kitchen. Mrs Appleby produced an old clothes-basket which they used when any weak or motherless baby lambs needed nursing indoors. Jane warmed a piece of old blanket and spread it in the basket.

'Now then, Tippy-boy —' Mr Appleby knelt beside the basket, and while Kitty raised the puppy's head, he opened Tippy's mouth and gently let some warm brandy and water trickle on to the back of his tongue.

Tippy gulped and coughed and spluttered. He opened his mouth for more and everybody chuckled.

'You know what's good for you, don't you, Tippy?' said Mr Appleby, giving him another spoonful. 'There's nothing like some brandy in water to put new life into any sick animal.'

At that moment Pete came in from the yard followed by Beauty. He was carrying a basket of bantam eggs.

'Hold Beauty, Pete,' Jane warned as the Alastian bitch pushed her way between them to the basket. 'Tippy's had a shock. He needs to be kept quiet.'

'Let her be,' advised Mr Appleby quietly.

Beauty padded up to the basket in which Tippy

lay. She put her head over the side of the basket, nosed her puppy inquiringly and then briskly began to lick him all over.

'Don't be so rough, Beauty!' Kitty scolded.

'She's doing the right thing,' said Mr Appleby. 'A mother-dog's lick is a good treatment for a sick puppy. Beauty's warming and comforting Tippy. She'll do him more good than any rubbing or massage we can give him.' He broke off to look up at his wife. 'How about getting lunch out of the oven? We'll all feel better after we've had a bite to eat.'

After lunch Mr Appleby said that Tippy should be given a chance to sleep quietly. So everyone left the kitchen – everyone, that is, except Beauty.

She insisted on staying with Tippy, sitting by the basket and occasionally giving the puppy's head a gentle lick. Skipper wanted to stay, too, but Mr Appleby took him with him to move the calves from the Home Meadow to Sunny Hollow.

'Will Tippy be all right, Daddy?' Kitty asked.

'I hope so, Kit,' Mr Appleby said.

'You're not really hopeful, Daddy. Oh, I ought not to have let it happen,' Kitty blamed herself. 'If Tippy doesn't get better it will be all my fault. How could I have been so stupid?'

'If Tippy hadn't jumped into the estuary he'd probably have misbehaved in some other way,' Mr Appleby sighed. 'We've done all we can for Tippy for the moment, so why not try to think about something else?'

'Oh, I can't,' Kitty protested.

'Can't you even think about that colt of yours?'

'Rusty?'

'Yes, why not give him a leading lesson?' her father suggested.

Kitty fetched a snaffle bridle, with a rubber bit, from the harness room and walked across to Lower Meadow where Rusty, her chestnut colt, was grazing with Dapple, his mother, and Prince and Darkie, the ponies belonging to Jane and Pete. Rusty was pleased to see her. He cantered across and nosed her blazer pocket in which were a couple of biscuits. They had been meant for elevenses that morning, but, when Tippy had jumped into the tide-race and nearly been drowned, she had forgotten them.

Rusty crunched the biscuits eagerly. Then Kitty bridled him and led him back to the farm. She tied him to the ring outside the stables and gave him a light brushing before picking up his feet in turn to get him used to having them handled. She was thinking of Tippy all the time. How was he now? Was he still sleeping? She left Rusty tied to a ring-bolt, and tiptoed to the kitchen window to peep inside. Yes, Tippy must be asleep. She could see his chest moving up and down while Beauty watched over him. Beauty looked drowsy, too. She stretched out her paws and lay down, her head resting against Tippy's basket as she fell asleep.

Kitty tiptoed away. Tippy sleeping was a good sign, she thought. When anyone was poorly her mother sometimes said that natural sleep did more good than bottles of medicine.

She untied Rusty who was getting impatient, and took him to the main road to get him used to being led through traffic.

The afternoon dragged, but at last it was tea-time and, having put Rusty back in the meadow, Kitty hurried to the kitchen. Tippy was sitting up in his basket while Mrs Appleby was heating some milk for him at the stove. Kitty crumbled a slice of bread, and mixed in a spoonful of sugar. Her mother added the lukewarm milk. Tippy climbed shakily over the edge of the basket. He sat down to eat his bread and milk. Then, evidently feeling stronger, he staggered to the hearthrug and lay in front of the fire.

When the Appleby family sat down to tea, Tippy moved to Mr Appleby's side to join Skipper and Beauty in waiting for scraps, their doggy gaze fixed hopefully on their master.

'Sitting up and taking nourishment, eh?' Mr Appleby said, spreading a piece of bread and butter with salmon-paste and dividing it into three for the dogs. He smiled at Kitty.

'It seems that we're going to rear Tippy after all, so you may as well start looking sunny again, chick!'

Chapter Five

A BIRTHDAY SURPRISE

TIPPY was snuffly for the next few days and his legs were still wobbly. Then suddenly he was his mischievous self again, but somehow his mischief did not seem to matter so much because everyone at Headland Farm was glad to see him full of life.

Mr Appleby had signed Kitty's card from the Sandbeach Port public library so Kitty borrowed a book called *YOUR DOG – its training and care.* Each day she gave Tippy a training session as the book advised.

The first lessons were quite simple – sitting when ordered, and walking to heel. Kitty pressed Tippy's hindquarters to the ground every time she said the word '*Sit!*' and Tippy soon realized what was wanted. Teaching him to stay sitting while she walked away was more difficult. Before she had gone a few paces Tippy would run after her, tail awag.

Steadily Tippy improved. Soon he stayed in the sitting position while Kitty crossed the yard. He would wait until she called him before bounding to her. He learned to walk to heel without pulling on the lead. He was intelligent, and it really seemed as if he was trying to understand what Kitty wanted. He very much wanted to please her.

Next day – a Wednesday in early August – began ordinarily enough, although, being Mrs Appleby's birthday, it was not really an ordinary day at all. As usual, Mr Appleby and Frank milked the cows before breakfast. Jane and Kitty fed and took fresh water to the hens and ducks and collected the eggs, while Pete attended to the bantams and rabbits.

Roddy fed the pigs, Captain, the big Shire horse, and the calves. Then the Appleby children ran through the Home Meadow to the next field where Prince, Dapple and Darkie, the family ponies, were grazing with Rusty.

Having seen that all was well with the livestock, the children went back to the house and found Mrs Appleby busy at the stove, cooking bacon and sausages. When she turned to serve them she found that the children had stacked their gifts by her place at the big kitchen-table.

Pete had bought a box of chocolates – the nut-centred kind which Mrs Appleby liked best. Kitty's package contained a bottle of eau-de-Cologne and a handkerchief with a lucky shamrock in the corner, while Roddy and Jane had put their money together to buy a smart, summer handbag.

Mr Appleby, as always, kept his present until last, and Kitty wondered what it could be, because he did not seem to be hiding anything. Then, with a grin, her father took a small buff envelope out of his pocket and handed it to Skipper, saying:

'Take this to your mistress.'

Kitty watched, puzzled, as Skipper padded to her mother's chair. What was Daddy's gift? Surely nothing exciting could be in that dull-looking envelope – yet Mummy seemed to think it was very exciting indeed. Her eyes twinkled and

she gave an exclamation of delight when she unfolded the piece of paper that was inside.

'You couldn't have thought of anything better, dear,' she told her husband, going across to kiss him.

Jane and Kitty, unable to contain their curiosity any longer, had left their places and were peering at the slip of paper.

'A receipt for the payment of the deposit on a washing machine!' Jane exclaimed. 'Fancy you keeping this a secret from Kitty and me, Daddy!'

'That's not the only thing I've been keeping secret,' said her father with a chuckle. 'I've planned another surprise for your mother's birthday. To-day's going to be a holiday for her.'

'Oh good for you, Dad!' Roddy approved.

'Yes, after breakfast Frank's wife's coming up to help him keep an eye on things here at the farm, and we're going to spend the day on the beach.' Mr Appleby put an arm round his wife and then looked at his children. 'We won't even trouble your mother to cut up sandwiches. We'll build a fire of driftwood, and we men —' he winked at Roddy and Pete — 'will cook ham and eggs, while you ladies —' he smiled at his daughters and his wife — 'just sit back and admire.'

'Yippeee!' whooped Pete.

'Hurrah!' cheered Kitty, and even Jane and

Roddy, who usually thought themselves too old to cheer, joined in.

Kitty never dreamt she would see the day when her father suggested taking a whole day's holiday off from the farm! Like most farmers he knew that there were always jobs and yet more jobs that needed to be done – often urgently – around the farm. This holiday idea showed that he must be pleased with everything.

And why not? thought Kitty. There had been a good hay-harvest and all the stacks had now been thatched.

The clover was cut and in the silo to make winter food for the cattle. They had had a second hay crop from the Seven Acre Field, and the corn was ripening well and would soon be ready for cutting. So, thought Kitty, with Frank, the cowman, and Gladys, his wife, keeping an eye on the farm animals and feeding them, perhaps it was natural enough that Daddy should feel like having a day on the beach with his family.

Soon the Appleby family – plus Skipper, Beauty and Tippy – were making their way over the headland to the beach. There was time for a swim before lunch and everyone went into the water, including Tippy, who needed some coaxing at first after his fright in the estuary. Kitty had found an old sorbo ball for Tippy to play with so that he did not make himself a nuisance by borrowing other people's.

Then, while Mrs Appleby and Jane and Kitty sunbathed, Mr Appleby and the two boys lit the fire and cooked the lunch. The dogs sat and watched, mouths watering as they sniffed the appetizing smell of frying, home-cured ham.

After lunch Mr Appleby snoozed comfortably, straw hat over his face, on Jane's lilo, while the rest of the family explored rock pools, looking for sea anemones.

Suddenly Kitty noticed some excitement farther along the beach. A crowd of children had gathered round a van.

Some small white dogs were jumping down from the back. There seemed to be six or seven of them, and they were followed by four miniature white poodles.

Kitty ran to see what was happening and caught sight of some lettering across the side of the van.

UNCLE DON AND HIS
PERFORMING DOGS

She turned and shouted to the rest of the family.

'It's a dog circus. Pete! Jane! Roddy! Mummy, wake Daddy! We mustn't miss this. Hurry, everybody. It's just going to start.'

Chapter Six

UNCLE DON'S DOGS

WITH Skipper, Beauty and Tippy bounding alongside, the Applebys hurried to see the dog circus. They took their places in the audience. Skipper and Beauty sat on either side of Mr Appleby, and Kitty held Tippy's collar to remind him that he must not get into mischief.

Everybody looked towards the man in charge of the dog circus. Kitty thought he looked a jolly sort of man. He was spry and blue-eyed, with a bushy white moustache and a bow tie.

'Hullo, boys and girls,' he greeted the onlookers. 'I'm Uncle Don and these are my performing dogs.'

'Hurrah!' cheered a small boy.

'This is going to be super,' Pete whispered to Kitty.

'We intend to give two performances a day —' Uncle Don went on. 'Morning and afternoon. So please tell all your friends.' He bowed and added: 'In just half a minute the performance will begin.'

The children watched with mounting excitement as Uncle Don went behind the van followed by all his dogs.

At last he appeared again and he carried several gaily-coloured tubs, three stools and a small stepladder on to the sands.

Uncle Don clapped his hands once.

'Pepi!' he called.

A small white dog wearing a red bow on his head and with a red and white frilly ruff round his neck bounded across the stage and ran up the stepladder to sit on the top.

'Bimbo,' called Uncle Don and a white dog in a green bow, and wearing a green and white ruff, took her place on one of the tubs.

'Mimi,' he called next, and a little dog with a pink bow and pink and white ruff ran across to sit on another tub.

'Fifi!' Uncle Don called.

Fifi's yellow bow bobbed gaily as she bounced across the 'stage', jumped on to one of the painted stools and immediately sat up in a begging position, her silky white paws neatly held in front of her yellow and white ruff.

'Gigi,' came Uncle Don's next call. A little white dog, with an orange bow and orange and white ruff, jumped on to the other stool.

Now only the tallest of the three tubs was left without a dog on it.

'Suki,' called Uncle Don and although everybody waited expectantly no dog appeared. 'Suki!' Uncle Don called again, and this time a perky little dog in a blue bow and blue and white ruff put his head round the van and then dodged back again.

'Suki!' Uncle Don sounded stern. 'Come here this minute.'

The little dog's head again came round the corner of the van. Suki hesitated a moment; then turned back and finally, as Uncle Don called him again, he trotted to his place with a tasty-looking bone in his mouth. Everybody laughed.

'So that's what was keeping you, Suki.' Uncle Don took the bone from the little dog. 'You can't do your act with a bone in your mouth. So I'll save it for you until the show's over.'

He picked up a hoop decorated with coloured ribbons and held it in front of Pepi who was on the step-ladder.

'Hoop-la!' he exclaimed.

As Pepi jumped through the hoop. Bimbo left his tub and ran up the step-ladder to take his place. Mimi moved into Bimbo's place and Fifi into Mimi's.

Kitty watched, fascinated. This was like a game of dog General Post. One after the other, faster and faster, the dogs scampered from tub to tub, and then to the step-ladder, taking their turns at jumping through the hoop.

The act was going well. The little dogs were jumping cleverly and there was a burst of applause as Fifi, having cleared the hoops, ran to the front of the 'stage' and sat up in front of the audience to beg. A small girl threw a chocolate to her. Fifi caught it in her mouth and chewed it delightedly while everybody applauded even louder.

This time, when Kitty took her hand off Tippy's collar to clap, the puppy was not content just to sit and watch. He wanted to join in. He had been watching the dogs closely and he thought he could do some of these tricks. Then everybody would clap him and say what a clever dog he was. He looked from Kitty to Mr Appleby.

Yes, Kitty and Master would be pleased with him!

So, before Kitty could stop him, Tippy bounded over the shoulders of two children who were sitting in front of him. The performing dogs were trying not to take any notice of distractions and even when Tippy joined them, most of them did not give him more than a sideways glance.

A gasp of surprise went up from the audience.

'Come back, Tippy!' urged Kitty, getting to her feet. 'Oh you silly puppy!'

'Gosh, Tip!' groaned Pete. 'Uncle Don was giving a super show and now you're going to spoil it.'

Chapter Seven

TIPPY'S NEW MASTER

FOLLOWED by Pete, Kitty edged her way past the other children, while Tippy scampered among the performing dogs spoiling the show.

'You naughty puppy!' Kitty exclaimed. 'I am sorry, Uncle Don.'

To Kitty's relief Uncle Don did not seem at all cross. Perhaps he was thinking that Tippy's sudden appearance helped to make the show more amusing.

The audience certainly thought so. The children chuckled and cheered. So Kitty and Pete stood beside the 'stage', and waited to see what Uncle Don wanted them to do.

'Tippy!' Kitty whispered urgently. 'Oh, please behave yourself.'

But Tippy did not hear. Ears quivering, he was listening to Uncle Don.

'So you want to jump through the hoop,' Uncle Don said to Tippy, 'and show everybody you're just as clever as my dogs.'

'Yes, please,' Tippy's wagging tail seemed to say: 'Yes, please.'

'Well, I dare say you are clever, Tippy,' Uncle Don added, 'but this hoop isn't big enough for you to jump through, you know. So why not wait there with your young master and mistress? Then, if you're good, I might let you join in the next act.'

'Yes, Tippy – come here!' Kitty pleaded.

Tippy moved towards her. Uncle Don held up the hoop again, and the small dogs started their routine of jumping through.

Before Kitty could stop Tippy he bounded in front of Mimi and the other dogs. Despite the fact that Uncle Don lowered the hoop, Tippy jumped right into it – and stuck, half-way!

'Oh, Tippy, you wouldn't listen to Uncle Don and now look at you,' Kitty groaned. All the Applebys ran on to the 'stage' to help.

Although the hoop was stuck round his middle, Tippy did not seem to mind. He wriggled with delight, while Jane held his front paws forward and Roddy tugged off the hoop.

'We're very sorry about this,' Mr Appleby apologized.

'Oh, don't mention it,' said Uncle Don.

'Tippy didn't mean any harm,' added Kitty, holding the puppy tightly by the collar. 'He just doesn't like to be left out of anything. He's a real show-off.'

'He's a born performer, if ever I've seen one,' Uncle Don declared, making Tippy beg for a cube of meat. 'A dog comedian!' He turned to the audience. 'I think we ought to see what else Tippy can do, don't you, children?'

'Yes,' chorused the children.

'Well, if you really want to, Uncle Don,' Mrs Appleby said doubtfully, and the Applebys went back into the audience.

Kitty watched, pleased that the performing dogs seemed interested in Tippy. She could see that they wanted to be friendly. They gathered round Tippy, jumping up, dodging under him and touching noses.

'This is going to be funny,' chuckled Pete as they sat down again. 'I wonder if Uncle Don knows how naughty Tippy can be.'

Next, Uncle Don tied coloured bows round the necks of all the dogs, red for one team and blue for the other. Tippy wore a red bow.

Uncle Don lined up the dogs – the red team at one side and the blue team at the other, and placed the big rubber ball in the middle. He blew a whistle, and all the dogs scurried for the ball. Tippy was the first to reach it. He tried to pick it up in his mouth, but it was too big, so, amid cheers, he nosed it forward, in and out of the other dogs and towards the far side of the van. Then the other dogs decided they were not going to let this newcomer have things all his own way, and Suki chased him and got the ball away between his front paws. Then the fun followed fast.

Pushing the ball with their paws and noses, the dogs sent it from one to the other. Once Pepi scored a 'goal'. Uncle Don blew his whistle, and sent the doggy 'players' back to their lines while he replaced the ball in the centre.

Tippy was enjoying the game. Even so, he was not quite sure that he was getting as much of the applause as he should. What could he do to make the audience laugh? Next time the ball came his way he managed to pick it up between his front paws and then to 'throw' it. The ball went over the heads of the other dogs, into the air and landed on top of Uncle Don's hat, denting it.

Uncle Don did not mind. While the children laughed and clapped he blew his whistle for a 'throw in' and gave the ball to Fifi, who cleverly held it between her paws and flicked it back into play.

At last the show was over. Everyone was thrilled. The audience had never seen such clever dogs.

Just then Uncle Don took his place in front of the van and said:

'If you have enjoyed our efforts to entertain you, please place your donations in the bags that my doggy assistants will bring.'

None of the Appleby children had any money with them, so Mr Appleby put in three shillings – sixpence each for all the family – because he thought it was such a good performance.

After the collection, the poodles trotted back to their master with the money bags.

Uncle Don put the money in the van. Tippy was the first to greet him as he came down the steps, putting his paws on the man's arm and jumping up to lick his face.

Although the performance was over, the children did not go away. They crowded round Uncle Don.

'What kind of dogs are these very small ones?' one boy asked.

'They're Maltese terriers,' said Uncle Don. 'They make fine performing dogs. They're easy to transport, and they're good at learning tricks.'

'Easier to transport than a pack of Alsatians would be,' said Roddy. 'You'd need a furniture van for them.'

'Yes,' nodded Uncle Don, looking towards Skipper, Beauty and Tippy. 'But I wouldn't mind one Alsatian in the troupe, if you happen to know of one.'

'Well, that's lucky,' exclaimed Roddy, 'because Tippy is for sale.'

'That's right,' Mr Appleby nodded. 'We've been trying to find a good home for him ever since he was eight weeks old.'

'Now that's very interesting,' said Uncle Don, and patted Tippy's head.

'We quickly sold all the other puppies of the litter,' added Mrs Appleby, 'but no dog-fancier wanted to buy Tippy because of the brown tip to his tail.'

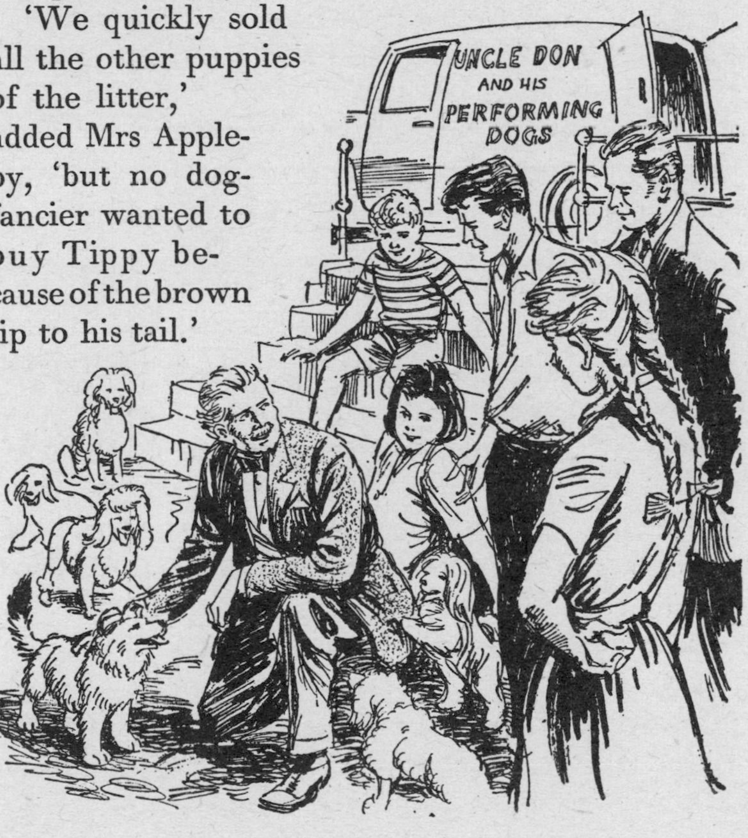

'And he was always in so much mischief that it didn't seem as if he would be any use as a farm dog,' Kitty added.

Uncle Don and the other children listened as the Applebys told the story of Tippy's short, but mostly mischievous, life.

'So nobody wanted to buy you, Tippy,' Uncle Don said kindly. 'Then it's lucky you met me, isn't it? Because I want you, and I value you even more because you're a bit of a clown. A dog clown is just what I need in this show.'

'Gosh!' gasped Pete. 'Do you really want Tippy to become a performing dog? Who'd have thought it?'

'Are you sure you mean it?' Mr Appleby asked Uncle Don. 'You'd like to have Tippy?'

'Certainly.' Uncle Don put a hand on Tippy's collar. 'How much will you take for him?'

Mrs Appleby spoke before her husband could say anything.

'Well, since we were once going to give him away, I don't think we ought to charge you very much, Uncle Don.'

'So we'll leave the price to you,' added Mr Appleby.

'I'd rather you named a figure,' said Uncle Don.

Mr and Mrs Appleby looked at each other and Mrs Appleby looked at Uncle Don and noticed that his suit, though neat and tidy, was threadbare in parts.

'Would a pound be too much?' she asked.

'Oh, Mummy,' said Roddy. 'Make it ten bob.'

'Ten shillings then,' said Mrs Appleby.

'No, I think I might be able to manage a pound.' Uncle Don delved into one pocket after another and produced various coins. Then he fetched the collecting bag from the van and counted out the remainder of the money. 'There, that's done it. No, I'm going to pay you a full pound,' he insisted as Mr Appleby protested. 'Tippy will be worth a lot more than that to me.'

The Applebys looked at each other uneasily. They all had noticed that Uncle Don had only a few shillings left after he had paid for Tippy. Of course he might have had more money somewhere else, in the van or at home, or at his lodgings if he had no home. Kitty felt she wanted to know more about Uncle Don and to befriend and help him.

'You said you'd be here for the rest of the season, didn't you?' she asked. 'So we'll be able to come and see your performance any time.'

When Uncle Don nodded, she added: 'It'll be fun to see how Tippy gets on as a dog clown. But – oh gosh! – we're going to miss him around the farm.'

Feeling sad at having to be parted from Tippy,

the children made a fuss of him. Skipper sensed that something unusual was happening. He stood in front of Tippy and barked, three or four times, right in the puppy's face as though he was trying to tell him that he was now on his own and must try to act like a responsible grown-up dog and to behave himself.

Then the Applebys set off for home.

As they climbed the zigzag path that led up to the headland, they looked back from time to time. Was Tippy watching them? Kitty wondered. And would he feel forsaken? No. Down there on the beach she could see that Uncle Don was feeding him. That would be to show Tippy that Uncle Don was now his master and that in future he would provide his meals. Tippy had found a good home – yet Kitty was feeling miserable!

'Tippy's lucky,' said Mrs Appleby. 'He's got a kind master, and though we're all sorry to lose him, we've got to make the best of it, so cheer up, Kitty. Try to smile, even if you don't feel like it!'

Chapter Eight

AT BACK CUSTOMS STREET

ALL that evening the Applebys wondered about Uncle Don – Tippy and the other dogs. Where were they living? They could not all be sleeping in the van.

At breakfast next day, Kitty said: 'I know we shall see Tippy on the beach at this morning's performance, but I'd like to find out where he spent last night and where he is now.'

Her mother nodded. 'I do wish one of us had thought to ask Uncle Don whether he had anywhere to stay.'

'Perhaps Uncle Don and the dogs could stay here,' Pete suggested brightly. 'That would be a super idea!'

'Don't you dare suggest such a thing to Uncle

Don.' His mother looked quite alarmed. 'Imagine fifteen dogs running round the farm. They'd put the hens off their lay, and upset the cows.'

'All the same,' said Kitty, 'I do wonder how Uncle Don is managing.'

Just then she got up from the table and ran out to meet Mr Jorkins, the postman, as he crossed the yard.

'I thought Mr Jorkins would know,' she said when she came back with two circulars and a bill in her hand, 'and he does. Uncle Don's rented an old shop half-way down Back Customs Street in Sandbeach Port. That's where he and the dogs are living.'

'I know the shop,' nodded Jane. 'The windows are boarded up. It's been empty for years.'

'I suppose Uncle Don must be sort of camping out there,' said Pete. 'How whizz!'

'I wonder if everything really is "whizz" for him,' Mrs Appleby said doubtfully. 'I think it might be a good idea if you children were to go down there after breakfast. You could take Uncle Don some eggs and farm butter.'

'Oh, may we?' said Kitty, hurriedly swallowing the last mouthful of bread and marmalade. 'We'll take Dapple and go in the trap.'

'We've certainly come to the right place,' Jane declared twenty minutes later as they drove down

Back Customs Street. 'Tippy must have heard Dapple's hoof-beats.'

'Yes – listen,' said Pete. Kitty, Pete and Jane recognized Tippy's yap. Then it seemed as though all the dogs in the Back Customs Street shop joined in, and grown-dog though he was, Skipper put his paws on the side of the trap and barked excitedly.

Jane halted Dapple by the kerb.

The children clambered down, and Kitty ran to knock on the shop door.

'Uncle Don'll never hear you above all that barking,' said Jane. She pressed down the latch and, opening the door, called: 'Are you there, Uncle Don?'

Kitty peered over Jane's shoulder.

Sunlight slanted through the doorway into the boarded-up shop, and there was Uncle Don, blinking and shading his eyes. He was just raising himself from a camp bed. He must have been lying down. Yet he was dressed and the bed was made with the blankets tucked under the mattress as though he had got up some time ago, and then decided to rest. Wasn't he feeling well?

Just then Tippy bounded to Kitty and, in the excitement of seeing him again, she forgot to ask Uncle Don why he had been lying down.

There was a scamper of many paws from a back

room and suddenly the children were surrounded by Maltese terriers and miniature white poodles. All the dogs were yapping, and it was a few minutes before any of the Applebys realized that something was amiss.

It was Jane who first noticed that Uncle Don had sunk down on an orange-box, his hands to his head, while Skipper was licking his cheek and whimpering.

'Oh, dear!' Jane exclaimed, hurrying to Uncle Don's side. 'You're not feeling well. What's wrong?'

'I thought you might be feeling poorly,' Kitty said, 'because you were lying down when we came in, weren't you?'

The three children gazed anxiously at Uncle Don as he slowly lifted his head. His face looked strangely sallow.

'I've been feeling off colour for the past month,' Uncle Don told them shakily, 'but never quite as badly as now.'

Jane put a hand to his head. 'I don't think you've got a temperature,' she said, 'but I can't be sure.'

'Do you hurt anywhere?' asked Pete.

'Well, no,' said Uncle Don. 'It's just that I feel queer.'

Kitty was about to say something, but Jane

interrupted her with big-sister firmness. 'I'm going to get a doctor,' she said, walking towards the door. 'That's what Mummy would do.'

Over an hour later Kitty, Pete and Jane were on the beach talking to a group of children who were waiting for Uncle Don and his dog circus to appear.

'Sorry, everybody,' Kitty announced. 'There won't be any show today.'

'And perhaps not tomorrow, either,' Pete said sadly. 'Perhaps not again this season.'

'Why not?' several children asked at once.

'Uncle Don's been taken ill,' Jane told them. 'We went to see him this morning, and he couldn't even stand up. So we got the doctor and he made us take the dogs into the back-yard while he examined Uncle Don.'

'Oh, dear. I hope it's nothing serious,' groaned one of the older girls.

'We don't know yet,' said Jane. 'The doctor didn't tell us anything. He just told us to sit quietly with Uncle Don while he got an ambulance.'

'So they've taken him away?' a little girl said in dismay.

Kitty nodded. 'Yes. He's in the Sandbeach Port General Hospital. He didn't want to go. He was worried about the dogs.'

'So we told him we'd look after them,' explained Jane. 'That's why we've come down here. We need volunteers to help us take them for a run. There are too many dogs for us to manage.'

All the children wanted to help.

'We've already fed them,' Kitty explained as they set off for the shop in Back Customs Street. 'And we shan't leave them by themselves to fret while Uncle Don's away. We telephoned Mummy and she says it will be all right for us to stay there most of the day.'

'And our big brother Roddy's going to sleep there at nights,' added Pete.

'Will we be able to go to the hospital and see Uncle Don?' one of the boys asked. 'I used to go twice a week when my dad was in there after he broke his leg.'

'I don't think Uncle Don'll be allowed many visitors,' said Jane. 'Not for a few days anyway.'

'Poor Uncle Don!' A girl with her hair in a pony-tail bow sighed. 'I do hope he'll be better soon. He's so kind and jolly – and all the dogs love him so much. They will miss him.'

Chapter Nine

HELPING UNCLE DON

KITTY, Pete, Jane, and the volunteers – almost all the children who had been waiting on the beach for the performance – hurried to the shop, and, using the leads that were hanging from hooks in the back room, took the dogs on to the sands with Skipper leading the procession.

Once let off the leads, Uncle Don's dogs ran wildly around as though searching for their master. Tippy also wanted to find Uncle Don, even though the kind man had been his master for such a short while. The Alsatian puppy jumped on a rock and looked all round the shore.

Although the dogs were disappointed and puzzled because their master had gone away, they nevertheless pranced around boisterously. Some of them did a few tricks for the children and then joined Skipper in a game of 'chase-my-tail'.

On the way back to the Back Customs Street shop they became excited and pulled at their leads, because they expected to see their master waiting for them. They searched and sniffed around the shop's back room and yard for trace of him, and when they realized he was not there they whimpered, and one of the Maltese terriers began to howl.

It was now nearly lunch-time, so Jane shepherded all the children out of the shop while Pete 'fielded' the dogs that tried to escape. In the street, Jane locked the door while Kitty shouted through the letter-box.

'Don't fret. You've got plenty of friends.'

'Yes,' added Pete. 'We're coming back. We shan't be long.'

During that day a number of children – including the Applebys – called at the hospital to inquire about Uncle Don. They were told that he was being X-rayed. No one – not even Mrs Appleby who called at the hospital after doing her shopping – was allowed to see him. So Mrs Appleby left a message that the children were looking after the dogs and that Roddy would be sleeping in the boarded-up shop. Next morning she telephoned the hospital and the ward sister said that Uncle Don would be allowed visitors for a short while that evening.

'Good!' said Kitty when she heard the news. 'I want to tell Uncle Don how I'm teaching Tippy to walk on his hind-legs!'

Neither Mr Appleby nor Roddy could go with the others to the hospital because they had to mend the milking machine which had broken down. So the rest of the family piled into the farm van with Mrs Appleby at the wheel. There was even room for Skipper.

When, a little later, Mrs Appleby parked the van outside the hospital Skipper jumped over the back of the seats and sat proudly in the front, with his fore paws on the steering-wheel, alertly looking through the wind-screen as though daring any stranger to touch his van.

Kitty had never visited anyone who was ill in hospital, and so she was quiet and subdued as her mother found the number of Uncle Don's ward from the inquiry desk. Then Mrs Appleby led the children down a long corridor and up some stairs to join other people who were sitting outside Ward 3M until the visiting bells rang as a signal for them to go in.

Several nurses passed them, brisk and calm about their work, and, inside the ward, Kitty could glimpse the dignified figure of the ward sister in her deep blue uniform dress, stiffly-starched white apron and frilled cap with its sister's 'strings' as badge of office. The door of a side-room marked *Ward Kitchen* opened and a pretty girl of about seventeen came out. She was wearing the lilac-print dress of a probationer nurse, and Jane and Kitty recognized her as one of the former sixth formers, and a prefect, at their school, who had left last term.

'Hullo!' she said when she saw the Applebys. 'I'm glad you could come. Uncle Don particularly wanted to see you. He's had one visitor today and he's got some news for you.'

'What sort of news?' asked Pete.

'He'll tell you himself,' said the young nurse.

'How is he?' Mrs Appleby inquired.

'Well, he's got to have an operation,' the nurse told them, 'but he's quite cheerful. He's a splendid patient. All the nurses love him, and I think it's wonderful how you've been helping him with the dogs.'

Just then a series of electric bells rang stridently.

'On your marks – go!' said Pete, and the Applebys moved forward with the other visitors as the ward sister pulled back the swing doors.

Uncle Don was in a bed half-way down the ward and Kitty felt relieved that he was propped up against his pillows and did not look so very ill any more.

'Well, every cloud has its silver lining,' Uncle Don greeted them. 'The doctor says that after a little while I'll be better than I've been for the last year, and I don't mind having the operation one bit. So there's no need for you all to stand there looking sorry for me. Here, Mrs Appleby,' he indicated the chair beside his bed. 'Make yourself comfortable.'

'I'm glad you're not worrying, Uncle Don,' Mrs Appleby said as she sat down.

'Because everything's under control,' added Pete. 'And all the dogs are well and Roddy doesn't mind sleeping there. Gosh! I wish I could sleep there too. Couldn't I, Mum?'

'We'll see,' Mrs Appleby said doubtfully.

'You've all been very kind.' Uncle Don's blue eyes were shining with gratitude. 'Friends in need. That's why I don't want to impose on you.'

'You're not doing that, Uncle Don,' Jane assured him.

'That's as may be,' said Uncle Don. 'When I was a lad I used to spend my holidays on my granddad's farm, and I know how you farmers are on the job from dawn to dusk at harvest-time. That's what I was worrying about while I was lying here, and then something happened this afternoon that seemed to make everything come right, after all.'

'Oh yes,' said Kitty. 'One of the nurses said that you'd got some news for us.'

'And so I have,' Uncle Don looked round at them all. 'News that's going to be quite a surprise to you.'

Chapter Ten

A SHADY CHARACTER

'PLEASE tell us your surprise, Uncle Don,' Kitty prompted, remembering just in time not to break the hospital rules by perching on his bed. 'We love surprises.'

'Is it about the dogs?' Pete asked eagerly.

'It is,' nodded Uncle Don. 'Right out of the blue it happened. This very afternoon a young man turned up at the hospital asking for me,' Uncle Don continued. 'I'd never set eyes on him before, but he knew all about me.'

'Who is he?' asked Kitty.

'Well, his name's Sid Hogan and he's been working at a fun fair at Brightsea,' Uncle Don told them. 'He'd had a difference of opinion with the proprietor. The fellow hadn't treated him at all well from what he said, long hours and small pay. Then just by chance he saw my poster about the dog circus and, having once worked in that line himself, he decided to come along and see the afternoon show and find out if I needed an assistant.'

'And instead he found out you were in hospital,' put in Jane.

'Yes,' Uncle Don nodded. 'And he came on the scene just when I need an assistant. He's going to look after the dogs and carry on with the performances. When I'm better we might go into partnership.'

'I hope you're doing right,' sighed Mrs Appleby. 'After all, this man is a stranger. How do you know he's trustworthy?'

'I take quite a lot of things on trust,' Uncle Don said cheerfully. 'It's my nature. Anyway, Sid Hogan told me all about himself. He used to be assistant to Serge Boroffsky who tours the music halls with some performing Pekes. Oh yes, Sid Hogan's had experience of looking after dogs, sure enough. He should be able to manage my troupe.'

'I see,' said Kitty. 'Your dogs are well trained, so they'll be sure to do what he wants them to, but how about Tippy? You know how naughty he can be. I think Sid Hogan may need our help until he gets used to Tippy.'

'Did you warn him about Tippy?' Jane asked.

'Well, no I forgot about that.'

'Don't worry,' Mrs Appleby told him. 'I'll explain everything to Mr Hogan.'

'Oh, do let us, Mummy,' begged Kitty. 'We want to see the dogs anyway. And I think we ought to make friends with Mr Hogan. There are dozens of ways we might be able to help.'

When the Applebys went back to the van, Kitty tried to persuade her mother to drive them to see Sid Hogan and the dogs right away.

'But it's almost Pete's bed-time,' Mrs Appleby protested.

'Bed-time!' scoffed Pete. 'What does bed-time matter for once? I haven't got to go to school tomorrow.'

'Very well,' sighed Mrs Appleby. 'But you children must not make yourself a nuisance to Mr Hogan.'

Five minutes later, she stopped the van outside the shop in Back Customs Street. Skipper was first out. He bounded across the pavement and dabbed at the door latch with his front paws. Above the boards that covered the lower half of the window Kitty could see the heads of leaping dogs.

Tippy, the poodles and the Maltese terriers wanted to see who had come to visit them!

The yapping became pandemonium when Mrs Appleby knocked at the door.

'I'm sure that we ought not to have come tonight,' she said to Jane. 'The dogs had probably settled down to sleep and we've disturbed them.'

A moment later there was the sound of a bolt being drawn back. The door opened a crack. The Applebys could not see anybody, but, through the opening, between the yapping, they heard a young man say almost gruffly:

'What is it? What d'ya want? Who's there?'

'We're friends of Uncle Don,' Mrs Appleby told him, through the half-inch crack. 'We've come straight from the hospital to see if you need any help.'

'Yes, you see Tippy used to be our dog,' added Kitty and, as she mentioned the puppy's name, a black nose wedged its way through the slightly open door. 'He can be very naughty. We wanted to warn you.'

'I dare say,' Sid Hogan grunted. 'Well, I may have taken on Uncle Don's dogs, but I hadn't bargained for a pack of kids as well.'

'We're quite useful!' protested Pete. 'We've

been feeding and exercising the dogs for Uncle Don.'

'And now you're upsetting them,' Sid Hogan pointed out rudely. 'Do me a favour, will you, and buzz off! I'm busy.'

Before the Applebys could say anything he had shut the door.

Kitty and the others stared in disappointment and dismay.

'Come along, children,' Mrs Appleby's voice sounded hurt as she turned to the van. 'We'd better go home.'

'Of all the rude, grumpy, horrid men!' Jane exclaimed, glaring back at the boarded-up shop.

'Unkind, too,' said Kitty. 'He doesn't sound at all the sort of man to be looking after dogs.'

'Of course, Sid Hogan might improve on acquaintance,' Jane said to the other Appleby children before breakfast next morning as they walked towards the orchard carrying water and corn for the hens. 'We ought to try to do our best to make friends with him for the dogs' sake.'

Kitty nodded. 'All the same,' she said thoughtfully, 'I don't think we ought to call at the shop again. He'd only get cross if we did.'

'Of course he would,' said Roddy, opening the door of the first poultry house and letting out the hens, while Jane carefully filled up the water troughs from the bucket. 'You can't blame him for being fed up last night – all of you barging along there and starting the dogs barking when he'd probably just got them settled for the night. I dare say the poor chap just wanted peace and quiet while he cooked his supper.'

'Could be.' Kitty still felt doubtful as she walked along the row of nest-boxes collecting the warm eggs from the hay-lined nests.

'I'll come with you this morning,' Roddy said. 'We'll go straight to the beach and see if we can help with the performance. Then I'll have a word with Sid Hogan and later pick up the sleeping kit that I left at the shop.'

'Good-oh!' cheered Pete, delighted at the thought of seeing Tippy and Uncle Don's other dogs so soon.

After breakfast Kitty caught and harnessed Dapple. The children climbed into the trap. Skipper jumped in after them and Roddy picked up the reins.

Dapple was soon pulling the trap along the Sandbeach promenade.

'That's odd,' said Kitty, scanning the sands. 'I can't see any sign of the dog circus.'

'Perhaps Mr Hogan's giving the show farther along the beach.' Roddy shook Dapple's reins and the grey pony's hooves clip-clopped as she trotted towards the pier.

They still could not see Sid Hogan or the dogs.

'Perhaps something's wrong,' Kitty wondered. 'I think we ought to go to the shop after all.'

For once Roddy and Jane agreed with their younger sister.

Pete looked up at Roddy.

'I'm glad you're with us,' he told his elder brother. 'Sid Hogan can be nasty, but you'll be able to stand up to him.'

Roddy did not answer. Kitty thought he looked grim. She knew he did not like arguments with people, but perhaps Sid Hogan would be more friendly this morning.

'Look!' Kitty gasped as, a few minutes later, Roddy turned Dapple into Back Customs Street.

The Appleby children stared at the scene ahead of them. Uncle Don's van was outside the boarded-up shop while a lanky young man (whom they deduced must be Sid Hogan) was shouting angrily at the six Maltese terriers which he held on leads.

'You little demons!' He jerked at the leads, his thin face twisted in anger. 'Get in that van.'

The dogs pulled in different directions. Some of them obviously wanted to set off for a scamper, while one or two seemed to be looking up and down for Uncle Don and were whimpering in a puzzled way. They knew Sid Hogan was not their master and they seemed to want to run away from him.

Roddy reined up Dapple, and the children saw the terriers make a sudden dash for freedom. Their leads crossed. They twisted round Sid Hogan's legs and, with a yell of fury, he fell sprawling to the road. At that moment the van doors burst open, and Tippy and the poodles bounded out. Full of life, Tippy dashed straight to Sid Hogan who was still on the ground. In a boisterous and friendly mood the Alsatian puppy put his front paws on the man's chest and gave his chin a quick lick. Sid Hogan, now completely losing his temper, let go of the terriers' leads long enough to slap Tippy hard on the nose.

'Hey, steady on!' Pete yelled. 'That's our Tippy!'

Chapter Eleven

RODDY VERSUS SID HOGAN

KITTY gripped her elder brother's arm as Sid Hogan hit Tippy again.

'Stop him, Roddy!' she begged.

'This is terrible!' Roddy said in a choked voice, pacing forward. He was flushed and angry, and he was holding himself in check as though he knew that to lose his temper would not be the best way to help Tippy.

'*Grrrrrr!*'

Skipper strained at his collar by which Jane was holding him back. To him, Tippy was still one of the family and he was not going to let any stranger take liberties.

Sid Hogan got to his feet and again hit Tippy who, with a yelp, broke away and, seeing the Applebys, ran towards them to be comforted.

'*Grrrrrr!*'

Now Skipper sounded really fierce, and Roddy had to help Jane to hold his collar to stop him from leaping at Sid Hogan and grabbing his sleeve between his teeth.

Sid Hogan stared angrily at Roddy who glared back at him. Meanwhile the Alsatian puppy fondly bunted Skipper and whined and whimpered, although his tail was wagging with delight. It was as though he were trying to tell the Applebys: 'I am glad to see you. I've had a dreadful time, and I thought you were never coming. Let's go home now.'

'Oh dear! Tippy still thinks he's our dog,' Kitty groaned. 'I wish he were!'

'He'd have been all right with Uncle Don,' said Pete, 'but now he's got a beastly man for a master.'

'Yes,' Kitty added. She walked up to Sid Hogan. 'You had no business to hit Tippy like that,' she told him. 'You're a big bully!'

'Leave this to me, Kitty,' Roddy said in his choked-up voice. 'A slanging match won't do any good.' He forced his tone to be polite. 'You don't know us, Mr Hogan, but we're friends of Uncle Don, and so we're interested in his dogs. My mother and sisters and brother called last night to see if they could help.'

Sid Hogan grunted. Then he seemed to think that he would be more clever if he appeared to be friendly. He gave a sly smile. 'You're friends of Uncle Don, are you? Well, that's different, I suppose. Any friends of Uncle Don are friends of mine. Sorry I lost my temper with that pup, but you see how it was. I'd been knocked sprawling, and I didn't stop to think what I was doing.'

'You hit him several times,' Roddy pointed out. Kitty was surprised how stern her brother sounded. 'That last blow was vicious. You might have injured him.'

Sid Hogan looked as though he would have liked to have slapped Roddy's face, but again he held his bad temper in check and, with a big effort, made himself sound apologetic. 'If I had, I'd have never forgiven myself.' His slyly whining voice made Kitty feel sick. 'Well, it won't happen again, and that's a promise. So what about us all being friends?' He held out his hand. Roddy hesitated. 'I've admitted I was in the wrong.' Now there was almost a wheedling note in Sid Hogan's voice. 'What more can I do? Come on. Shake!'

Kitty watched her elder brother hesitate. She could see that Roddy still did not trust Sid Hogan.

'Oh, for goodness sake, shake hands, Roddy,' Jane said impatiently. 'What does it matter, anyway?'

His expression wooden, Roddy put out his hand and Sid Hogan grasped it. He pump-handled Roddy's hand for quite a time and then, to add to poor Roddy's wretchedness, he thumped him heartily on the shoulder.

'There! Now we're all friends and there are no hard feelings,' he declared, 'and to prove it, I'll take you up on your offer to help me.'

'Help?' Roddy asked blankly, playing for time now that Sid Hogan had out-manœuvred him by cunning. 'In what way?'

'Why, to give me a hand with these dogs, of course. I want to get them all into this van and I can't do it single-handed. They're so lively this morning.'

'Whizzo!' whooped Pete, the only one of the Appleby family to be taken in by Sid Hogan's falsely-friendly manner. 'This is just what we hoped for. We'll be able to come along to the beach and lend a hand with the show.'

'You'd have to come a long way to do that, sonny,' the young man told him. 'I'm not giving any performances here in this dead-and-alive place. I want bigger audiences and more lolly. I'm off to Brightmouth where the crowds are.'

'Brightmouth!' Kitty echoed in dismay, looking up from stroking Tippy who was nuzzling her hand. 'But that's over fifty miles away and we never go there, so we might never see Tippy again.'

Roddy squared his shoulders and looked Sid Hogan right in his shifty eyes.

'Does Uncle Don know that you're taking his dogs away from Sandbeach?' he asked.

'Know?' the young man echoed slowly as though playing for time while he thought out the next move. 'Of course. Didn't he tell you when you saw him in the hospital?'

'He didn't say anything about it,' Jane said definitely.

'Well, fancy that!' the young man exclaimed. 'I am surprised. But p'raps it slipped his mind. Yes, I suppose he'd be thinking about this operation of his, poor chap.'

He looked from one to another of the four Applebys. 'Well, how about giving me a hand with these dogs?'

The children gazed at each other doubtfully. They knew that Sid Hogan was bad-tempered and crafty. Probably he was a liar as well. They couldn't believe that Uncle Don knew of his intention to take the dogs away from Sandbeach and that he had given his permission.

Kitty glanced up at Roddy and tried to read his thoughts. He was frowning, playing for time, wondering if there was any way they could match Sid Hogan's cunning by cleverness of their own.

But what could they do? Call a policeman? Or try to get in touch with Uncle Don at the hospital? But there was no time. Sidney Hogan was about to leave any minute, in fact as soon as he got the dogs into the van. So, why help him?

'Well, make up your minds,' Sid Hogan said roughly, and then shrugged. 'Suit yourself.' His tone was now sarcastic. 'Sid Hogan doesn't have to ask for favours from a bunch of kids. Those dogs'll come sharp enough into the van for something to eat. Yes, it's lucky I haven't had time to feed them yet this morning. . . . Here, watch.'

He opened the passenger-seat door and brought out an old biscuit tin. As he took off the lid the dogs surged round him, and Tippy rose from Kitty's side to join the others.

The dogs followed Sid Hogan to the back of the van, scrabbling at his legs, trying to get at the tin.

'See!' Sid Hogan said to the Applebys. 'They love their Uncle Sid.'

He delved into the tin and scattered dog biscuits over the floor of the van. Tippy was the first to jump inside, but the other dogs were only half a bound behind and Sid Hogan slammed shut the doors.

'All done by kindness,' he said to the children, turning the handle of the door to fasten it. 'Trust Uncle Sid!'

Kitty's eyes were bright with rage as she stormed: 'You're a horrid man and I hate you!'

'That makes me want to weep!' Sid Hogan said with a mocking chuckle. He climbed into the van. 'Well, kids, thanks for nothing! I don't suppose I'll be seeing you again, I hope.'

Speechless with anger, the Applebys stared after the van. Skipper was angry, too. He did not know what it was all about, but he sensed that there was trouble.

While the children had been talking to Sid Hogan, a growl had risen in the big Alastian's throat every time the young man had spoken in a nasty tone or had gone near Tippy. Skipper had stopped growling when Sid Hogan had produced the dog biscuits, but now he realized that the young man was driving off and taking Tippy and the other dogs with him, he felt more fierce than ever.

So jerking his collar from Roddy's grasp and,

growling and barking in turn, Skipper streaked after the van, which was now disappearing round the corner into the main road.

'Skipper!' Roddy shouted. 'Come here!'

Hearing Roddy's command, Skipper paused at the corner and looked back at the children. He wanted to obey Roddy, but, on the other hand, he did not want to let Sid Hogan take Tippy away. If only he could make the children understand.

'Woof! Woof!' he barked towards them as though to let them know that he could not come back until he had rescued Tippy.

Dapple pawed the tarmac, impatient to be on the move.

'Climb in!' Roddy told the others as he jumped into the trap and picked up Dapple's reins. 'We'll go after Skipper, though we haven't much chance of catching up with him; I can't let Dapple gallop on these tarmac roads.'

The other Applebys clambered into the trap and Dapple set off at a ready trot. When they reached the main road there was no sign of Skipper or the van, so Roddy turned Dapple towards Brightmouth.

'The trouble is that we don't even know whether Sid Hogan was speaking the truth when he said he was going to Brightmouth.' Roddy shook the reins, urging Dapple to trot faster. 'But as both he and Skipper are out of sight, we've no choice but to go in this direction. If he's taken any other way goodness knows where Skipper may have got to.'

Kitty groaned because the traffic lights showed red as they approached. Now they would have to wait for them to change to green. By now Skipper must be a long way ahead. Kitty felt impatient, and, to delay them further, the traffic was bad in the Market Square. However, Roddy skilfully guided Dapple through it, and soon they were out of the town and bowling along the main Brightmouth road at a smart pace.

Past the filling station and the road-house café they went and still no sight of Skipper. Then they were into the open country and Dapple shied once or twice at the shadows of trees on the road. They swung over the pack-horse bridge and turned the corner towards Dilbury Common. Kitty never once took her eyes off the road hoping to see Skipper's familiar white shape ahead. When at last she did, she could scarcely believe her eyes. Yes, the weary padding dog was Skipper sure enough. But he was not heading to Brightmouth as the Applebys had expected. He was coming towards them, plodding along dejectedly, head down and tongue lolling. He looked tired and dispirited.

When he saw the Applebys, he perked up. He seemed to forget his tiredness. His tail waved and he gave a pleased bark.

The children jumped from the trap and ran to meet their dog, while Dapple dropped her head to graze at the roadside.

'Poor old chap!' consoled Roddy, fondling Skipper's head. 'You're certainly pleased to see us. All the same, I suppose you're disappointed because you weren't able to rescue Tippy all by yourself.'

Kitty and Pete knelt on the grass to hug the big dog.

'I wonder what happened,' said Jane. 'Why did Skipper turn back?'

'Well, he'd soon have lost sight of the van,' deduced Roddy, 'but that didn't stop him gamely running on. He'd have gone on until he dropped as long as he was sure he was going in the right direction.'

'That's it!' exclaimed Kitty as she lifted Skipper's paws in turn and with her handkerchief dusted the road-grit from between the pads. 'He must have got to the five crossways, and then he didn't know which road to take.'

Jane nodded.

'So he realized he needed our help after all. Probably he wished he'd never dashed off without us,' she added, and bent down, looking into Skipper's puzzled eyes. 'You did wrong to run off like that, Skipper, but we forgive you, so try to cheer up.'

'Come on, everybody!' Roddy urged. 'It's past lunch-time. We ought to get back or Mum will start worrying. Get in, Skipper.'

The children climbed into the trap and Skipper jumped in after them willingly but, when he saw that Roddy was turning Dapple round and heading back towards Sandbeach, he tugged at Roddy's arm.

'Behave yourself, Skipper.' Roddy spoke sharply. 'How can I drive Dapple with you biting my sleeve?'

Skipper let go. He moved to the back of the trap and, putting his nose over the tail-board, looked back along the Brightmouth road and whined. He

knew that with every hoof-beat, Dapple was taking them away from Tippy.

'Don't fret, Skipper.' Kitty knelt on the floor of the trap to comfort him. 'You've done your bit. If it hadn't been for you we'd never have been sure that Sid Hogan really was heading for Brightmouth, and had not just told us that he was in order to put us off the scent.'

'That's all very well,' said Jane, stroking the Alsatian's head. 'But what Skipper's really worrying about is why we're going home now instead of making straight for Brightmouth to rescue Tippy. Skipper thinks we've deserted his pup.'

'But we haven't!' Kitty said definitely, and then darted a quick glance at her elder brother. 'Have we, Roddy?'

'Somehow or other—' Roddy's tone was determined — 'we'll stop Sid Hogan from cheating Uncle Don, and being cruel to Tippy and the other dogs. We'd go straight on to Brightmouth now if it wasn't too far for Dapple. Besides, this is one of those tricky times when we need Dad's help.'

'Good for Daddy!' exclaimed Kitty. 'And good for you, Roddy!'

'Woof!' barked Skipper to add his own opinion, and then, as he remembered how Sid Hogan had treated Tippy: '*Grrr! Grrr! GRRR!*'

Chapter Twelve

MR APPLEBY DECIDES

'NOW don't bother your father any more about Uncle Don's dogs,' Mrs Appleby told the children before breakfast next morning. 'We talked it all over after you'd gone to bed last night.'

'And isn't Daddy going to do anything?' Kitty asked, looking up from stacking sliced bread on a plate. 'We felt sure he'd help.'

'And he will,' Mrs Appleby said definitely. 'He is going to do something. But, first he's got to be sure of his facts – whether Uncle Don did give his permission for Sid Hogan to take the dogs away, for instance.'

'That's true,' agreed Roddy who, with Pete, was in the yard, scraping mud off the family's wellingtons. He spoke through the window. 'And the only person who can tell him is Uncle Don.'

'And he's being operated on today,' sighed Kitty, 'and it may be days before we can see him.'

'Golly, yes!' Pete's freckled face was anxious at the window. 'He'll be feeling so rotten that he won't be able to be bothered about anything.'

'And we'll have to be careful not to ask questions that might start him worrying,' added Jane, laying two knives, a fork and a spoon at each member of the family's place at the table.

'Start who worrying about what?' asked Mr Appleby, coming into the house after his before-breakfast round of the farm.

'Uncle Don about the dogs, and that horrid Sid Hogan,' explained Kitty, putting the cornflakes near her father's dish. 'But we're not going to bother you about that. We know you'll do your best to tackle Sid Hogan, and put things right.'

Jane nodded and said:

'Just as you did about that greedy business man who tricked you into letting him put caravans on Puffin Point. Then we had to help rescue people when the caravans were hit by a gale in the middle of the night.'

'You were terrific then, Dad.' Pete gazed up at his father. 'A super-Dad!'

Everyone laughed despite the fact that they were worried.

'It seems as though you've a lot to live up to, dear,' Mrs Appleby told her husband.

Mr Appleby nodded as he poured some corn-flakes on to his dish. 'The trouble is that I hate rows. I'm the peaceful type, I suppose. But one thing's certain: Uncle Don can't look after his own interests just now. So we'll have to watch them for him.' He glanced round at his family. 'Yes, children, we'll help somehow.'

To everyone's relief Uncle Don's operation was a success and he progressed so quickly that, on the third day, he was allowed to have visitors.

Not having heard from Sid Hogan, he was eager to have news of his dogs, and his eyes twinkled as the Applebys stood around his bed. He looked so pleased that Kitty felt particularly sorry that her father had to break some news that might be upsetting to him.

As quietly and gently as possible Mr Appleby told the invalid that Sid Hogan had taken the dogs from the old shop in Back Customs Street to Brightmouth.

'Why should he do that?' Uncle Don looked puzzled, and the twinkle faded from his eyes. 'Oh dear! If I hadn't been feeling so poorly and been at my wits' end to know what to do for the best, I wouldn't have taken him on without finding out more about him.'

'Don't worry yet, Uncle Don,' Mrs Appleby tried to reassure him. 'We're all driving over to Brightmouth tomorrow and we'll make sure that the dogs are all right.'

Then everybody tried to make light of the

whole matter, and, for the rest of the visit, Sid Hogan, the dogs and Tippy were not mentioned.

'Oh, we are lucky to have a Daddy like you.' Kitty impulsively hugged her father next morning as he opened the back door of the van for the children to pile in. 'I am glad you're going to take us to Brightmouth. You love Tippy and Uncle Don's other dogs just as much as we do. Everything will be all right now that you're going to take charge. Mr Hogan will have to behave himself when you turn up.'

'I'll do my best, chick,' Mr Appleby said, patting her shoulder. 'But first I want to find out the lie of the land. I want to make sure of my facts before I act.'

'You'll see the facts, right enough, Dad,' said Pete, making room in the back of the van for Skipper. 'That's it, Skip!' He patted the big dog. 'Dad's going to rescue Tippy and settle Sid Hogan. Yippeee! Brightmouth, here we come!'

'Don't speak too soon, Pete,' Roddy groaned as he glanced towards the lane. 'If you see what I can see you'll realize we may not be going to Brightmouth after all this morning!'

Kitty's heart sank as she followed her elder brother's gaze. Round the bend came a tractor pulling a huge piece of farm machinery.

'The combine harvester!' she gasped in dismay. 'Oh, no! It can't be. Not this morning. It was supposed to be going to Seven Trees Farm before it came to us. Oh, Daddy, tell the men to take it away. Tell them the barley isn't ready for cutting. Tell them to come back next week.'

'I wish I could,' Mr Appleby sighed, getting out of the van, 'but I can't turn the combine harvester away. The barley's ripe and the sooner it's safely cut and carried the better in case the weather should break.'

'That's true,' Roddy had to agree.

'Barley's queer stuff, you know,' went on Mr Appleby. 'It's just right for cutting at the moment and we should get top price for it from the brewers. But if we left it and the weather broke we'd never get it properly dry and then it would have to go for cattle food – and half my year's farm profit would go with it. If I didn't take my turn now that the men have brought the harvester I might have to wait for weeks. It's a stroke of luck that the gang have come here before going to Seven Trees.'

Roddy climbed resignedly out of the van, but Pete did not budge. He turned to Mrs Appleby who was in the front passenger seat. 'You take us, Mum,' he coaxed. 'You drive the van just as well as Dad does and you'll be able to tell Mr Hogan a thing or two.'

'Sorry, Pete.' Mrs Appleby also got out of the van. 'I shall be needed here. Somebody's got to feed the harvesting gang and make their tea, you know.'

'It's no use,' sighed Jane. 'And we shan't be able to go tomorrow either. It'll take two days to harvest those five big fields.'

'Don't give up like that, Jane.' Kitty was anguished. 'Goodness knows what may be happening to poor Tippy – and to Mimi and Fifi and the poodles, and the other terriers, too. Sid Hogan's a horrible man.'

'Yes,' agreed Pete. 'He may be beating them or

starving them or anything. We've got to do something today, Dad.'

'Very well,' Mr Appleby said, turning to face the children. 'Your mother and I can't take you to Brightmouth, so you'll have to go by yourselves.' He took out his wallet, and handed Roddy a pound note and a ten-shilling note. 'Here you are, Roddy. This should pay for the coach fare and your meals. Now don't tackle Hogan yourself or start any trouble. Watch him; notice how things are and then you can tell me all about it tonight.'

'Very well, Dad.' Roddy put the money away safely.

He glanced at his watch. 'Jiminy! The Creamline Coach goes past the lane-end in five minutes. Come on, Kit—' He caught his sister's arm before she hugged her father again, 'no time for that. Jane, Pete, Skipper – we've got to hurry.'

'Don't forget your macs!' Mrs Appleby dived into the back of the van and handed out the raincoats. 'Off you go, then, and take care!'

The four Appleby children set off at a run, out of the farm gate and down the lane towards the cross-roads with Skipper bounding ahead. They had to jump on to the hedge-bank to pass the combine harvester which almost filled the roadway. They arrived at the cross-roads, panting and winded, but just in time to catch the Creamline long-distance coach.

Later that morning Roddy, Jane, Kitty and Pete, with Skipper on the lead, were hurrying along the busy promenade at Brightmouth. Near the main jetty they could see Uncle Don's van drawn up with a crowd of children apparently watching Sid Hogan and the performing dogs.

Skipper could scent Tippy and the other dogs, and he was pulling at the lead. Pete was about to let him go, but Roddy put a hand on his young brother's arm.

'Don't let him off, Pete!' he warned. 'We don't want him to bound up to Tippy in the middle of the performance and spoil Sid Hogan's show. Dad said we weren't to cause any trouble, remember.'

'Right-ho, Roddy.' Pete tightened his hold on the Alastian's lead. 'That's it, Skip! Keep to heel! Heel! Back! Good dog!'

Jane paused and looked ahead, listening. 'From the sound of that audience nothing could spoil Sid Hogan's show. Those children aren't clapping or laughing. They're actually jeering! Listen!'

Chapter Thirteen

WHAT A DOG CIRCUS!

'*BOO!* Yah! *Booh!* Muffed it!'

As they got nearer the Applebys heard the jeers of the children who were watching the dog circus.

Sid Hogan had painted out the words UNCLE DON on the van. Instead, he had put the words: UNCLE SID'S DOG CIRCUS.

'It isn't really a dog circus any more,' Pete said, looking from one of the performing dogs to another hoping to see Tippy. 'It's a washout.'

'I'd hate to have Sid Hogan as an uncle!' Jane said feelingly.

'So would most of these children, judging by the jeers,' said Roddy.

Kitty was not sure whether she was pleased or sorry. One thing was certain, the show was an absolute flop. The dogs would not work for 'Uncle' Sid.

The Applebys reached the edge of the crowd and Kitty was about to push through when Roddy caught her arm.

'Tippy's just made a so-called entrance,' he said. 'Don't talk loudly.' He turned to Pete who was holding Skipper. 'Keep Skipper quiet, Pete. I don't want Tippy to see us, because if he did he'd dash from the stage and so warn Sid Hogan that we're on the warpath.'

So Kitty stood on tiptoe to watch over the shoulders of a bigger girl in front. There was Tippy, looking puzzled and unhappy, his brown-tipped tail drooping so that it looked as though it hadn't a wag left in it.

He was staring at a hoop which Sid Hogan was holding for him to jump through. Tippy did not jump. Instead he bit at the hoop trying to pull it out of Sid Hogan's hand. Next moment they were having a tug-of-war.

Tippy seemed brighter. He looked as if he were enjoying this. But Sid Hogan wasn't. Kitty bit back a shout of protest as Sid Hogan, exasperated, cuffed Tippy.

'Boo!' jeered some of the children.

'Silly Uncle Sid!' taunted a boy who was near the front. 'He can't make his dogs do anything right!'

Just then Tippy jerked the hoop from Sid Hogan's grasp and scampered with it round the van.

His brown-tipped tail streamed behind – an invitation to the other dogs to chase him.

Impatiently Sid Hogan took off his hat and flipped at any dog that scampered within flipping distance.

Kitty turned to her elder brother. 'Stop him, Roddy. Don't let him hit them. He's a beastly man!'

Roddy forced himself to keep calm. 'I don't think he's really hurting them this time, and we promised Dad that we wouldn't cause any trouble.'

'Yes,' added Jane. 'We're here to watch and report—'

Jane broke off and flinched as Sid Hogan hit Tippy a blow with his hand that really did seem to hurt. Tippy yelped. The Applebys gasped in dismay, Roddy's fists clenched and a growl rose in Skipper's throat. The big Alsatian strained at his lead.

'Stop it, Skip!' Pete begged, as Skipper's collar slipped from his grasp. 'Help, Roddy!'

Roddy dived and managed to get a grip on the collar. 'Steady, Skipper! Quiet. Sit down!'

Skipper tried to obey Roddy, but he simply could not stop growling. '*Grr! Grrrr! Grrr!*'

'Good gracious!' exclaimed the girl in front of Kitty. 'Your dog does sound savage. Is he safe?'

'Quite safe,' said Kitty. 'It's just that he doesn't like the way Sid Hogan treats those dogs.'

'He's a horrid man,' said the girl.

'Yes, and I bet he doesn't give the dogs enough to eat,' put in the girl's brother. 'I brought them some scraps from the hotel yesterday. You'd have thought they were half-starving.'

'Where does Hogan keep the dogs?' Roddy asked, watching Sid Hogan chivvying the dogs into the van after having decided to abandon the performance.

The boy shook his head. 'I'm not sure, but he always drives along the Marine Terrace and up Cliff Road. He must keep them somewhere along there, I suppose.'

'I'm surprised he keeps on with the performances,' put in a woman who was standing beside Jane. 'It can't pay him. The dogs do their tricks so badly that it makes people disinclined to give.'

A small boy joined in, with an impish grin: 'I put a couple of pebbles in the collecting bag yesterday,' he told them. 'I don't mind bringing bits for the dogs, but I draw the line at giving my pocket-money to that rotter!'

At that moment Sid lifted the last of the dogs into the van and slammed the doors. The Applebys withdrew behind a breakwater, so that Sid Hogan would not see them. They flinched when they heard a protesting whine from Tippy as he drove off. Skipper heard the whine, too, and nearly jerked his lead from Pete's and Roddy's grasp as he tried to follow the van.

'What do we do now?' Jane asked, patting Skipper to calm him.

'We'll stay to see the performance this afternoon, and see if the same thing happens,' decided Roddy. 'Then we'll telephone Dad and report.'

The Applebys had lunch in a snack-bar – sausages, chips and tomato sauce – went on the pier, and then waited, in vain, on the sands for Sid Hogan to appear with the dogs.

'He must have got fed up after this morning's rotten show,' said Roddy. 'So we'll see if we can find the place where he's keeping the dogs, and have a snoop round there.'

'One boy said that he always goes along Cliff Road,' said Jane. She went up to some children who were making a sand fort and asked if they knew where Sid Hogan kept the dogs. A youth in blue jeans and a yellow shirt told Roddy that he had seen the dog-circus van parked at night along Cliff Road outside a disused railway coach that had once served as the pavilion of some long overgrown tennis-courts.

'Come on!' Roddy said grimly, and, with Skipper eager for action, the four Applebys hurried along the promenade. They went past the boating lake and the roller-skating rink until they came to Cliff Road. It rose quite steeply between rows of bungalows and at last they came to a group of four big houses, standing screened by trees. Farther on they saw a disused quarry, bounded by a hedge but, through a five-barred gate, the children could see a derelict hard-tennis-court, grass-grown and weedy with broken wire-netting hanging from the leaning posts that surrounded it. On its side in the hedge bottom lay a board with the faded lettering:

CLIFF ROAD HARD TENNIS COURTS

Set back against the quarry face was a ram-shackle railway coach, its paint peeling and blistered.

There was no sign of Sid Hogan or the van, but from inside the railway coach came the yapping and whimpering of Uncle Don's performing dogs.

'This is the place,' said Roddy as Skipper gave a meaning whimper. 'Now watch your step, everybody – and if we run into Hogan let me do the talking.'

They hurried through the gateway to the rail-way carriage and Kitty rubbed clean a patch of grimy window-pane so that she could see inside.

In the carriage Tippy, the Maltese terriers and the miniature poodles were padding round and round, sniffing at the sides and doors, as if they were trying to find a way of escape. Kitty could see no signs of food, and though there was a water-bowl on the floor it was empty.

'It's a shame!' Kitty said indignantly as Jane, Roddy and Pete crowded to see inside. 'Sid Hogan

has no right to be keeping Tippy and Uncle Don's other dogs in such a horrid way.'

At that moment Tippy saw her and jumped up to the window-pane. Skipper saw the puppy and put his front paws on the door-handle so that he could look through the pane. Tippy's breath was misting the glass on one side and Skipper's on the other and both their tails were wagging. Kitty knew that they wanted to get to each other to romp.

Suddenly, Skipper's tail stopped wagging and he turned from the window with a growl.

Kitty spun round to see the dog-van turn into the gateway. Sid Hogan was at the wheel, and she could see that he was staring at them. He seemed surprised, but not at all dismayed. Kitty glared. Sid Hogan was actually smiling at them all, in an unpleasant, mocking way.

Chapter Fourteen

RODDY'S MYSTERY

SKIPPER sprang forward, a growl rising in his throat.

'Quick, Roddy,' Kitty warned. 'Grab him!'

Roddy grasped Skipper's collar and had to hold on to it with both hands. Skipper was trying to get at Sid Hogan who, quite unperturbed, stepped out of the van and looked at then sneeringly.

'Bad-tempered dog you've got there!' he said. 'You ought to get him a muzzle.'

'He's only fierce with nasty types like you!' Pete flashed. 'And then he wouldn't bite. He'd only hold.'

'Well, you hold on to him unless you want me to have you run in for keeping a dangerous dog,' Sid Hogan warned. When he saw that Roddy had control of Skipper, he looked relieved, and added: 'So we meet again do we? And what brings you all here, may I ask?' He glared. 'As if I didn't know! I suppose you've come to look at your precious Tippy and the other so-called performing dogs.'

'They performed well enough for Uncle Don,'

Jane retorted. 'You can't expect them to work for you when you don't treat them properly.'

'They'll work for me before I've done with them.' Sid Hogan's jaw tightened. 'I'll either lick 'em into shape or I'll sell 'em. I'll get something back for my trouble before I've done.'

'Sell them!' Kitty echoed. 'But they're not yours to sell. Those dogs belong to Uncle Don.'

'They belong to me.' Sid Hogan's smile was triumphant. 'And I've got a receipt to prove it.'

Roddy was scornful. 'I suppose you tricked Uncle Don into signing some trumped-up paper or other when he was feeling ill.'

'His signature's on it!' Sid Hogan hedged. 'I'll show you.'

He felt in his wallet pocket and brought out a slip of paper. Pete tried to grab it, and Sid tantalizingly held it out of reach. As he did so something dropped to the ground. Sid must have brought it out of his pocket with the paper. Roddy noticed it and looked thoughtful, but the others were too interested in Sid's 'receipt' to see what the unpleasant young man had dropped.

'Come on, Rod!' Pete groaned, his freckled face flushed with anger. 'Let's mob him. Now's our chance. Let's get that receipt. Then we can 'phone Dad and ask him to bring a cattle truck to take the dogs away.'

'Now then!' Sid backed away. 'I warn you! I'll have the law on you all.'

'Give me that paper!' Kitty said, jumping to try to snatch it from Sid's hand.

Skipper strained to get from Roddy's grasp. He had been growling non-stop ever since Sid came on the scene, and now Roddy had to hold his collar with both hands to stop him attacking Sid.

'Let Skipper go, Roddy,' Pete urged. 'Let him bite the rotter. He deserves it.'

'Stop this, all of you!' Roddy ordered, suddenly stern. 'We promised Dad not to cause any trouble. Now come along; we're going to catch that 'bus. We'll report all this to Dad, and let him deal with it.'

'But the 'bus doesn't go for another hour,' protested Kitty.

'We can't go tamely home and let Sid Hogan get away with this,' Jane said. 'He hasn't even fed the dogs.'

'Let Skipper get him, Roddy, please!' begged Pete.

'We're going to the 'bus,' Roddy said stolidly. 'Come on, you three. That's an order.'

'Yes, big brother knows best,' mocked Sid Hogan. 'So do what he tells you.'

'Oh, you!' gasped Pete.

Then, unwillingly, the younger Applebys

obeyed their elder brother. With Skipper looking back and growling and with Tippy yelping pitifully from the railway coach, they followed Roddy to the road.

'You're the limit, Roddy!' Kitty groaned. 'It's not like you to give in.'

'We can't just go away, like a lot of cowards!' protested Jane. 'It would be letting Tippy down.'

Pete tugged at his elder brother's sleeve. 'Come back, Rod, please. We're more than a match for that Hogan. Let's have a show-down and rescue Tippy right away.'

'Be quiet, all of you,' Roddy urged in a low voice, going farther down the road and signalling to them towards the ditch behind a clump of gorse. 'Use your brains. Quiet, Skipper!'

He put his hand over the dog's jaws to silence him.

Jane stared at Roddy.

'What's all the mystery?' she demanded.

'Yippeee!' breathed Pete before his brother could answer. 'You've got some plan, Rod. I might have known you would have.'

'What are we hiding here for?' Kitty was puzzled. 'And why are you being so mysterious?'

'I haven't time to explain now,' Roddy whispered. 'I want to see what Sid Hogan's going to do next, but I don't want him to see us.'

'The coast's clear,' Kitty whispered back, her gaze on the quarry. 'He thinks we've gone to the 'bus.'

'He's coming to the gate to make sure,' said Jane as Sid Hogan looked up and down the road and then walked briskly away from them along the road.

As he disappeared round a bend, Roddy gave Pete a nudge. 'You're the smallest, Pete. Creep along the ditch and watch where he's making for. Don't let him see you.'

Ears pricked, Skipper, with the other children, watched the youngest Appleby run along the ditch in a crouching position. At the bend of the road, Pete stealthily crept forward. Then he dodged back and signalled to the others. When they reached the bend, Sid Hogan was out of sight.

'Which way did he go, Pete?' Roddy asked.

'I can't quite be sure,' admitted Pete. 'First he went towards the houses on the cliff edge, and then he somehow disappeared.'

'Never mind.' Roddy patted Pete's shoulder. 'You've done jolly well.'

'I think Skipper knows which way he went,' Kitty said. 'Let him track Sid, Roddy.'

'Not yet,' Roddy held tightly on to the lead, while they all walked towards the houses where Pete had last seen Sid Hogan.

The houses were white-painted and sunny-looking, situated just off the road overlooking the cliffs and the beach and facing their own lawns and beds of roses to the sea beyond. Each house was separated from the next one by high overlap fencing.

'I wish you'd tell us what you're up to, Rod!' sighed Pete.

'I think I know,' guessed Jane.

'You'll all soon know,' Roddy said, and although his face was tense with strain, he gave a slow smile.

Deftly he unbuckled Skipper's lead, but still held the dog by the collar.

'All in good time, Skipper,' he said. 'But it might spoil everything if I let you go too soon.' He looked at his wrist-watch. 'We'll give Hogan a couple of minutes. By that time he ought to have started his shady job.'

'Oh, Roddy!' Kitty exclaimed, exasperated, but she could not get a word out of her elder brother as he intently stared at the second hand of his watch.

'Now!' he said, and released his hold on Skipper's collar.

With a deep-throated growl, Skipper bounded forward. He quested, nose to the ground, darted to the first gate, and ran along the fence. He leapt over a low part where a gale had blown down the top half of the fencing. Then he streaked across a lawn towards the house, disappearing from view behind some tamarisks.

'Come on,' Roddy urged. 'After him! Quickly!'

Chapter Fifteen

WELL DONE, SKIPPER!

SKIPPER sped across the lawn. He cleared a flower border in one magnificent leap and bounded to the french window.

'*Grrrrrr!*'

He was hot on the trail. He reared up, put his paws on the window catch and the window swung open. In a second he was inside the room, and snarling at a figure bent over the drawers of a desk which had been forced open.

On the floor lay a litter of papers. Ink spread on the carpet in a pool from a smashed ink bottle. Sticks of sealing wax, envelopes and writing-paper lay beside it. Skipper hurled himself at his enemy – the man who had been unkind to Tippy.

The Appleby children reached the open french window in time to see Sid Hogan raise an arm to protect his face as Skipper jumped at him. He went down beneath Skipper's weight.

'Help!' Sid Hogan was scared. As Skipper's front paws held his shoulders to the ground and the white Alsatian lowered his face to growl near

Sid Hogan's throat, he pleaded. 'Get him off! He'll kill me!'

'He won't,' said Kitty. 'Skipper's only holding you. He won't bite unless you try to get away. You're a bad man. You broke into this house to steal.'

'Yes,' said Pete, 'and Skipper's going to teach you the lesson you deserve.'

'Grrrrrr!' Skipper snarled. '*Grrrrrrrrr!*'

'Please help!' Sid Hogan begged. 'Call him off.'

'Not likely,' Roddy said. His gaze swept round the room. 'Jane, there's a telephone on that table. Get the Brightmouth police. Tell them where we are and ask them to come quickly because we've caught a thief. Then telephone Dad and tell him that we've missed the coach. Explain what's happened.'

While Jane was telephoning, the others stood in a semi-circle, watching Sid Hogan closely in case he should try to throw off Skipper's grip. Sid did not move an inch. As for Skipper, he was glad to be allowed to give the bullying Sid Hogan the scare that he deserved. Every time that Sid Hogan looked as if he might be going to move, Skipper gave another menacing growl and showed his teeth.

Kitty looked admiringly at her elder brother. 'Roddy, you're a wonder,' she declared. 'Did you really know that Sid Hogan was going to break into a house and if so, how?'

Roddy tried to be modest. 'It was nothing really,' he said, 'but you know that Scotland Yard book I got from the library – well, it said that thieves often use thin strips of celluloid to open spring locks. Hogan dropped a strip of celluloid from his pocket when he showed us that so-called "receipt" he said Uncle Don had signed.'

'And you put two and two together and guessed what he was going to do,' Pete prompted.

'Yes, but I didn't know which house he'd got his eye on,' Roddy explained. 'Skipper must have the credit for leading us here. I expect Hogan had been watching this house for a day or two and knew when the owners would be away.'

'Too clever by half, you are,' Sid groaned. 'Just when I'd got everything fixed lovely, too. The folks have gone off to Italy for a holiday. I thought I'd do the job by daylight so that I could see what to pinch without having to shine a torch around the place.'

Kitty still looked puzzled. She turned to Roddy. 'You said the celluloid must have been to open a spring lock, but the french window hasn't got a spring lock.'

Roddy glanced at Sid Hogan

'Well?'

'I didn't need to use the 'loid. I busted a pantry window.'

'I see,' nodded Roddy. 'Then you opened the french window so that it would give you an escape route for a quick get-away. You've a nerve, I must say – entering by daylight. I expect you thought you wouldn't be seen because the house is screened by bushes and high fences.'

Before Sid could reply they heard the crunch of fast-moving tyres on the gravel drive outside.

'The police!' Kitty announced, and as Skipper took his gaze off Sid Hogan, she added: 'Your job's

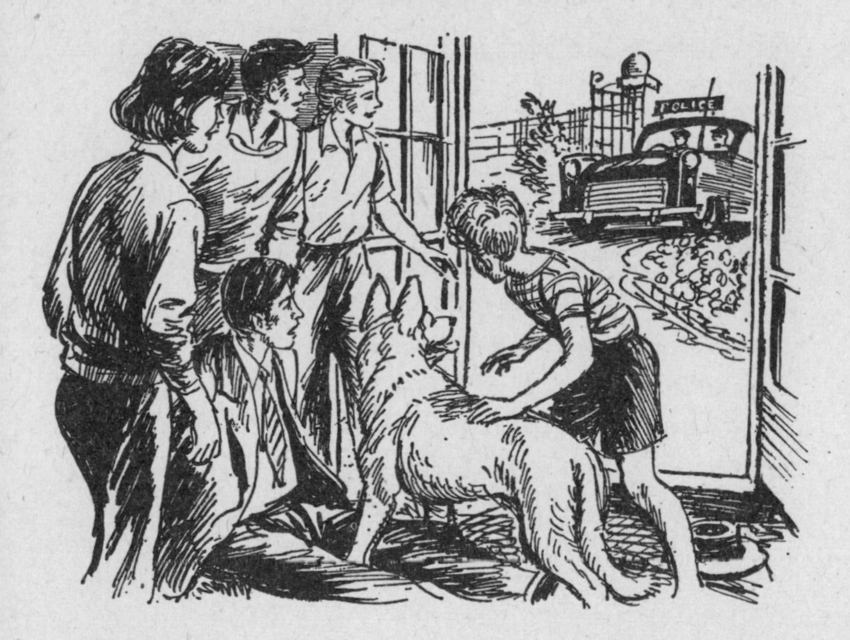

done now, Skip, old boy, and jolly well done, too.'

A few weeks later, the Appleby family, together with Uncle Don, all his dogs – including Tippy – and Skipper and Beauty too – were enjoying a picnic on the beach.

Uncle Don had just given his first performance since his operation. He had received a wonderful welcome from the holiday-makers, and now to complete his happiness, the Applebys had produced a huge picnic basket to share with him and his dogs.

Uncle Don looked fit and jolly as he sat against a breakwater, eating sandwiches, with Tippy on one side and Skipper on the other. He seemed as though he hadn't a care in the world now, thought Kitty.

And he hadn't. During his last few days in hospital, the Appleby children had cleaned out the shop in Back Customs Street, tacked some dog photographs on the wall, and put up some flowered cotton curtains that Jane had sewn on her mother's machine. They had made the place look homy. Roddy had painted out Sid Hogan's name on the van and replaced it with Uncle Don's.

They did not even talk about Sid Hogan any more. He had faded into the background like a bad dream. He had been convicted, and sent to prison.

And, as it turned out, he had been sent to prison twice before – once for stealing and once for obtaining money by false pretences, and, before that, he had twice been on probation.

It was odd though, thought Kitty, sharing part of her egg sandwich with Suki. Liar and cheat though Sid Hogan was, he had not been lying when he said he had worked with other performing dogs.

The police had made inquiries and discovered that he had, for a time, behaved quite well as assistant to the foreign 'Professor' and his performing Pekinese. Then the Professor discovered some money had disappeared – and so had Sid Hogan.

I suppose he must have liked dogs in a way, Kitty thought to herself. But he just hadn't enough patience to train or look after them properly. If he hadn't liked dogs at all, he wouldn't have bothered about Uncle Don's – or did he just seize the opportunity of tricking Uncle Don out of them when he was ill —?

Kitty felt Tippy bunt against her arm.

'Penny for your thoughts, Kitty,' Uncle Don was saying and Kitty looked up, smiled, and then glanced towards Tippy and Skipper who were running in circles over the sands, playing chase-my-tail.

'I was thinking,' said Kitty, 'that every summer

we'll be able to have at least one picnic like this – all of us, and you and all the dogs, Uncle Don, because you'll have to bring your dog circus to Sandbeach every season.'

'Yes, of course,' agreed Mrs Appleby, looking at Uncle Don. 'The holiday-makers will expect it.'

'And so will Skipper!' added Pete. 'He wouldn't want to lose touch with Tippy. He'll want to see for himself year by year just how Tippy shapes.'

'Skipper and son!' Kitty exclaimed as the two dogs romped together. 'Aren't they good pals?'

'I'll be here with you every summer from now on,' Uncle Don vowed, and looking round at the Applebys, he added happily: 'Among real friends.'

STAY ON

Here are details of other exciting TARGET titles. If you cannot obtain these books from your local bookshop, or newsagent, write to the address below listing the titles you would like and enclosing cheque or postal order—*not* currency—including 7p per book to cover packing and postage; 2–4 books, 5p per copy; 5–8 books, 4p per copy.

TARGET BOOKS,
Universal-Tandem Publishing Co.,
14 Gloucester Road,
London SW7 4RD

SKIPPER AND THE RUNAWAY BOY 35p

Judith M. Berrisford

0 426 10719 5

The Appleby children were frantic! If *only* Pete and Kitty had told someone about Tim, the mystery boy they had found and hidden in the cottage on Puffin Point! Now he was marooned on Bird Island with his dog, Chummy, and Pete and Kitty were too afraid to tell the truth because Tim was wanted by the police! Once again, Skipper, their lovable Alsatian dog, comes to the rescue and saves the day. *Illustrated.*

SKIPPER—THE DOG FROM THE SEA 30p

Judith M. Berrisford

0 426 10487 0 **Target Animal Fiction**

A strange white Alsatian dog visits the Appleby seaside farmstead by moonlight. Whose dog is he? Will he make friends with the four Appleby children—Roddy, Jane, Kitty and Pete? What is the mystery behind him? The Appleby family have some exciting moments in this thrilling story before they find the answers to these questions. . . . *The first adventure in this famous series. Illustrated.*

SKIPPER TO THE RESCUE! 30p

Judith M. Berrisford

0 426 10495 1 **Target Animal Fiction**

Bad news! The Appleby farmstead is in danger of having to be sold off, so it's Skipper, Roddy, Jane, Kitty and Pete—to the rescue! Whilst the children are busy trying to raise money to help the farm out of its difficulties, Skipper does a little extra rescue work of his own and ends up winning the Blue Cross Medal! . . . *The second adventure in this famous series. Illustrated.*

WELL MET BY WITCHLIGHT 30p

Nina Beachcroft

0 426 10356 4 **A Target Adventure**

In which Sarah, Christopher and Lucy meet a strange little old woman called Mary, a 'white' witch who can tame animals, raise wind and water, change her shape and, yes—actually fly on a broomstick! Whether or not she can deal with the evil-eyed Mrs Bella Black, a very powerful 'black' witch who lives in the next village, is another matter which concerns the children very much as they are caught up into the middle of a terrifyingly dangerous battle fought out between the two witches on the supernatural plane.

DOCTOR WHO AND THE CYBERMEN 35p

Gerry Davis

0 426 10575 3

THE CYBERMEN have arrived. With metal limbs, they have the strength of ten men. They can live in the airless vacuum of space. They have no heart, no feelings, no emotions, and only one goal – power! In the year 2070, a small blue planet caught their attention. They would land, attack, ransack, destroy and finally abandon . . . Can DOCTOR WHO save the Earth and defeat an enemy whose threat is almost as great as that of the mighty Daleks? *Illustrated.*

DOCTOR WHO AND THE CURSE OF PELADON 30p

Brian Hayles

0 426 10452 8

What is the secret behind the mysterious killings on the Planet of Peladon? Is Aggedor, Royal Beast and Protector of the Kingdom, seeking a deadly revenge? Can DOCTOR WHO escape the claws of the mighty Aggedor and discover the truth? *Illustrated.*

SEA-GREEN MAGIC 30p

Elisabeth Beresford

0 426 10479 x **A Target Adventure**

In which Johnny finds a funny, square-shaped bottle with a strange misty look about it whilst exploring sea-side rock pools. Imprisoned inside is an Arabian Djinn, or genie, who when released is destined to create some awkward problems for Johnny, Lorna and Alan. *Illustrated.*

PETER PIPPIN'S 3rd BOOK OF PUZZLES 30p

0 426 10348 3

Thousands turn to Peter Pippin's Puzzle Corner every week in newspapers all over the country. Here is anothe rfascinating collection for all the family to enjoy. Amusing EYE-CATCHERS and WORD GAMES pack the pages,and there are dozens of PICTORIAL CROSSWORDS. *A marvellous companion for journeys and holidays.*

If you enjoyed this book and would like to have information sent you about other TARGET titles, write to the address below.

You will also receive:

A FREE TARGET BADGE!

Based on the TARGET BOOKS symbol—see front cover of this book—this attractive three-colour badge, pinned to your blazer-lapel or jumper, will excite the interest and comment of all your friends!

and you will be further entitled to:

FREE ENTRY INTO THE TARGET DRAW!

All you have to do is cut off the coupon beneath, write on it your name and address in *block capitals*, and pin it to your letter. Twice a year, in June and December, coupons will be drawn 'from the hat' and the winner will receive a complete year's set of TARGET books.

Write to:

TARGET BOOKS,
Universal-Tandem
Publishing Co.
14, Gloucester Road,
London SW7 4RD

If you live in New Zealand, write to:

TARGET BOOKS,
Whitcoulls Ltd.,
111, Cashel Street,
Christchurch

If you live in South Africa, write to:

TARGET BOOKS,
Purnell & Sons,
505, C.N.A. Building,
110, Commissioner Street,
Johannesburg

If you live in Australia, write to:

TARGET BOOKS,
Rical Enterprises Pty. Ltd.,
Daking House,
11, Rawson Place,
Sydney, N.S. Wales 2000

——————————— cut here ———————————

Full name..

Address..

....

....

Age..............................

PLEASE ENCLOSE A SELF-ADDRESSED ENVELOPE WITH YOUR COUPON.